T0194345

THE JOURNEY OF
Christopher

THE JOURNEY OF
Christopher

MICHAEL J. DISALVO

WESTBOW
PRESS®
A DIVISION OF THOMAS NELSON
& ZONDERVAN

WestBow Press books may be ordered through booksellers or by contacting:

WestBow Press
A Division of Thomas Nelson & Zondervan
1663 Liberty Drive
Bloomington, IN 47403
www.westbowpress.com
1 (866) 928-1240

Because of the dynamic nature of the Internet, any web addresses or links contained in this book may have changed since publication and may no longer be valid. The views expressed in this work are solely those of the author and do not necessarily reflect the views of the publisher, and the publisher hereby disclaims any responsibility for them.

Any people depicted in stock imagery provided by Getty Images are models, and such images are being used for illustrative purposes only. Certain stock imagery © Getty Images.

This is a work of fiction. All of the characters, names, incidents, organizations, and dialogue in this novel are either the products of the author's imagination or are used fictitiously.

ISBN: 978-1-9736-6370-6 (sc)
ISBN: 978-1-9736-6372-0 (hc)
ISBN: 978-1-9736-6371-3 (e)

Library of Congress Control Number: 2019906221

Print information available on the last page.

WestBow Press rev. date: 6/10/2019

CONTENTS

To my beautiful wife, my journey would not be complete without you. To my Godson Daniel, don't ever give up on your dreams. And, in loving memory of my mother who loved Christmas more than anyone.

PROLOGUE

P EOPLE HAVE ASKED THE FOLLOWING common question for hundreds of years: Are we really alone in this life? This question can have two different meanings. First, are we alone on this planet, or is there other life somewhere in the universe? Second, are we alone, or is God out there watching over us? Timeless debates have taken place over both interpretations. But what if the answer to both meanings is the same? What if we aren't alone in either sense of the meaning?

One young man had an experience that led him to the answer to this age-old question. He faced a voyage he neither was prepared for nor expected. The adventure tested him in ways he had never been tested before. Mentally, physically, and emotionally, the brave lad was put through vigorous trials that would have challenged the best of men. Most of all, the quest challenged him spiritually, with only two possible outcomes: defeat or inspiration. His experience has come to be known as *The Journey of Christopher*.

CHAPTER 1

Meet the Family

IT WAS A COLD, GRAY, AND SNOWY Saturday morning in the great midwestern city of Chicago. The beautiful metropolis in Illinois had many nicknames, such as the City of Broad Shoulders, Second City, and Chi-Town. People were already outside, fighting the winter weather. Few things in life were as bone-chilling as the way the Chicago wind could cut through a person. The winter weather led one to remember perhaps the most famous nickname for the city: the Windy City. The gusts and gales could make one feel alive and take one's breath away at the same time. It was not uncommon to see people duck around a corner or behind a building just to get a short break from the frigid breeze.

That day, more people were braving the polar-like air than normal, for it was the last day of shopping before Christmas Eve. All the stores were full of Christmas trees and lights, and carols played overhead to assure everyone it was that wondrous time of year. Windows were full of the hottest new shopping items of the season, and the elaborate displays themselves were worth fighting the cold weather to see. There was always something special and magical about Christmas in the big city.

Young Christopher walked into the enormous mall with his family. His mother, Mary, lived for that time of year. Wrapping presents, decorating the house, baking cookies, and picking out the perfect gifts for people gave her a smile that could light up the entire city. Though she had a jolly personality throughout the year, it reached new heights during Christmastime. While she was a fan of all holidays, Christmas was by far her favorite. Few things made her happier or filled her with more pride than having Christmas for the whole extended family at her house. She had a way of making everyone feel special, and it came effortlessly to her. If her family was happy, she was happy.

Christopher's father, Michael, was a loving, caring, and generous man. He was smart, with knowledge on a wide variety of subjects, but he was not the type to act superior to anyone. He epitomized the cliché of what a man from Chicago should have been: hardworking, blue collar, and strong yet compassionate.

Unfortunately, Michael's sentiment toward that time of year differed from Mary's. It was a sad time for Michael, as every Christmas song he heard reminded him of how fast the years were going by. His parents, who had both passed away, also had possessed a love and joy for Christmas that had been second to none. With them gone and some of his brothers and sisters now spread across the country, he felt nostalgic about Christmases past, when the whole family had been together to celebrate the holidays. It seemed families too often moved farther away from each other, as making a living sometimes got in the way of making a life.

Christopher's younger brother, Joey, was only six years old, and he saw Christmas as the greatest time of year. As most children his age knew, as long as he had been good all year, Santa Claus would bring him the special toy he wanted. Joey was the one most involved when Mary decorated the tree and baked cookies. He saw how happy his mom was during that time, and the cheer was contagious. As much as Joey loved both of his parents, the biggest influence in his life was his older brother, Christopher.

Christopher had just turned sixteen years old. A role model in almost every way, Christopher was someone his younger brother, Joey, could be happy to look up to and aspire to be like. Christopher was an intelligent, strong, street-smart young man who was never afraid to speak his mind. He was well respected among his peers, as he was known as a person who would stand up for what he believed in. He was always quick to step in to defend someone when he saw an injustice happening. Being a teenager growing up in the city, he saw injustice usually in the form of bullies picking on weaker kids. Bullying, of course, could take on numerous appearances, ranging from verbal abuse to stealing to violent attacks and assaults. Christopher was always the first one to step in to protect a weaker kid who had fallen under an undeserved attack. That, of course, had led to a lot of confrontations and fights throughout his young life. Over the years, however, he always had held his own in those altercations, and he had gained a certain reputation in the neighborhood. Now those confrontations were less common, as people usually backed down when Christopher got involved. They did so not only out of fear but also out of respect. He had paid his dues and earned his stripes.

Christopher was a smart kid, although his report cards from school didn't provide any evidence to support that claim. Christopher always got into trouble with his teachers for not completing homework or talking too much in the classroom. Christopher had never been fond of homework because it cut into his time spent playing sports or hanging out with his friends. His behavior frustrated his teachers and his parents to no end. He received an A on almost every test he took. However, due to the lack of homework completion, he usually ended up with Cs in school. Everyone who knew Christopher felt that average grades were far below his potential. Christopher knew that he wasn't applying himself fully, and it was something he strived to change one day.

Despite his academic shortcomings, Christopher had always possessed a positive attitude about things and was outgoing. People were naturally drawn to his fun personality and enjoyed interacting and conversing with him. Unfortunately, that type of bonding with others was not encouraged in the classrooms. Even though the teachers were sometimes upset that he interrupted their class time, he had a way of always making everyone laugh that made it easy for the teachers to forgive him. He was good for the morale in the classroom because his levity helped to brighten the moods of both students and faculty. Compared to other problems educators in the city faced, an outgoing young man with a knack for lifting people's spirits was not the worst thing to have to deal with, especially in light of the ever-growing problem of drugs and weapons, which seemed to be infiltrating schools with younger and younger kids each year. Every teacher wished that a student like Christopher was the biggest problem in his or her classroom.

About a year and a half ago, Christopher had made his confirmation. In a family like Christopher's, confirmation was a big deal. Confirmation involved a young man or woman confirming belief in God and Jesus and vowing to keep the commandments as set forth in the Bible. The faith given in baptism was confirmed and made strong. Christopher was proud after making his confirmation, and his faith was indeed strong.

Only a short time after, his paternal grandmother, Michael's mother, had passed away. Her death had struck the family, including Christopher, hard, as she had been one of the greatest women in the world to them. Christopher found it confusing that the two events had happened so close together and, thus, had had a hard time getting into the Christmas spirit the past couple years. He had always been mature for his age and had always had a passion for understanding things. Growing up, he had learned quickly how respected Michael was among family and friends. Whenever Michael talked, people listened. Michael always made Christopher feel that his opinion mattered, which fueled Christopher's desire to learn. Christopher always was considerate of other people's feelings, and he had an insight beyond his years into what made people happy.

Insight could be hazardous sometimes; because Christopher was so insightful, he possessed a realistic attitude. As good as he was at reading other people and their feelings, he had a logical and detached approach, rather than an emotional approach, to situations in life. He had developed a narrow "Seeing is believing" attitude, as he looked at everything in life with a black-and-white state of mind. There was no gray, in his opinion, in some discussions. When his grandmother's health had deteriorated and she had passed away, Christopher had not believed it was God's will, as some at her funeral had said. He knew she had died because she was older and had been a smoker for years. That was it to him—the plain and simple truth. There was no other majestic reason or secret plan as to why she had died. There was no higher power involved that had played a role in taking her away from his family, just as there was no secret wizard hiding behind the curtain. Her body simply had given out the way a car did if the owner didn't change the oil or transmission fluid. It was a realistic attitude and approach to life but not a happy one for such a young person to have.

Christopher did not want to be shopping with his family that morning. It was Saturday, and it was snowing outside. In his mind, that was ideal football weather. A natural athlete, Christopher enjoyed most sports, especially the big three of basketball, baseball, and football. However, football was his all-around favorite. Christopher loved everything about football; he had been watching the Chicago Bears play for as long as he could remember. Michael had shown him videos of all the Bears greats, including legendary players Gayle

Sayers, Dick Butkus, Walter Payton, and Brian Urlacher. Christopher immediately had been hooked on the game and on the experience of watching it with his dad. There was something special about the fact that there were only sixteen games in an NFL season, and the family loved watching them all. It was one of their favorite things to do together, and now even his younger brother was starting to understand the game, which made it even more fun to watch. He loved to watch football almost as much as he liked to play the game. Luckily, he knew that most of his friends were probably also out shopping or home sleeping at that time, so he tried to make the best of being there at the mall. Still, he would rather have been throwing the football around than shopping for Christmas presents.

Not only was Christopher having a difficult time getting into the Christmas spirit that year, but he was also starting to question his belief in the whole holiday. Recently, his history class had discussed that December 25 was not actually the true birth date of Jesus Christ. December had not even been a month on the calendar back in that time, and historians had tried to estimate the approximate time of Jesus's birth and decided on December. Christopher was starting to think the whole celebration was nothing more than a clever lie. Santa Claus wasn't portrayed accurately, and it wasn't really Jesus's birthday. He wondered what was real about the holiday.

However, the emotional side of him remembered the special feeling he had gotten during Christmastime when he was younger. He remembered that warm, cozy feeling and wondered why he didn't feel it anymore. Maybe the love and joy that his mother, Mary, gave had created such a feeling. Maybe the whole extended family being together and the presence of his grandmother had made the holidays that much more special as he was growing up. Now that he was older, he thought the coziness of the holiday he used to feel was nothing more than a sentimental feeling. He thought maybe it was just a feeling of pure emotional attachment that wasn't logical or factual.

"What's wrong, Christopher? Aren't you excited to be shopping?" Mary asked.

"Sure, Ma, it's just that nobody can look as excited as you do," Christopher responded.

"Oh, you know your mother too well," Mary said with a smile.

Michael then said, "You know guys just don't get into shopping as much as girls do, Mary."

"I know, honey," Mary responded, rolling her eyes in a loving way. "But it's the last day of shopping before Christmas Eve. I have an idea. Why don't we split up so we can finish faster? Then you two can get home to do your guy stuff. Joey can come with me and help me pick out last-minute gifts. Okay, Joey?"

"Okay, Mommy," Joey replied with a smile.

Mary always knew how to make Joey feel special and included. "Let's all meet in the front of the mall exactly three hours from now."

"Three hours?" Michael said. "Seriously? You can't possibly have that many gifts to still buy. I know you start Christmas shopping in September. Do we really need that long?"

"Maybe longer. There's always fun in finding those last-minute gifts you didn't know you needed. But we'll meet then to see if everyone is done," she said with a smile and a laugh.

The family went their separate ways to finish their last-minute shopping. Christopher figured that since he had to be at the mall instead of outside playing football, he might as well go to the arcade to play some video games. It wasn't the same as playing a real sport, but it still had the competitive feel he loved. One of the main reasons Christopher liked that mall was because of the arcade. Arcades were no longer as commonplace as they used to be in malls, but that mall still had a huge arcade with a wide selection of games to choose from. He was able to play video football, video basketball, fighting games, shooting games, and racing games— the selections were endless.

Three hours could fly by for a young man playing video games, and before he knew it, the time to meet up with his family had already come and gone. He ran out of the arcade and hurried to meet them at the front of the mall. When he arrived, they were already there. Everyone was holding shopping bags, even little Joey—except for him.

"Where are your bags, Christopher?" his mom asked, looking confused.

He wondered how to answer without admitting he hadn't even looked in a store. It would have broken her heart to know he didn't care that it was Christmastime. He didn't want to hurt her feelings or ruin her good time that way.

"I didn't really find anything that I liked, Ma. Don't worry, though; Santa will bring everyone what they want. Right, Joey?" Christopher asked, trying to take the attention off himself.

"That's right!" Joey shouted with excitement.

Mary left the conversation at that but gave Christopher a look that almost made him feel ashamed. "Well, I guess we're done shopping then. Let's take Joey to see Santa, and then we can head on home," she said.

Michael and Christopher agreed, and they all headed to the center of the mall so Joey could see Santa. While Mary and Joey waited in line, Michael and Christopher sat on a bench away from the hyperactive crowd. Michael made sure to sit in a spot where he could keep an eye on his wife and son, though. Not only did he want to make sure they were protected, but he also did not want to miss the expression on Joey's face when his eyes lit up at the sight of jolly old Saint Nick. Michael lived for his family, and as long as they were happy and safe, he was happy. That was why he knew something was wrong with Christopher.

"So what were you really doing for the past three hours, Chris? Talking to girls or playing video games?" the father asked the son.

"What makes you say that, Dad?"

"Because I know you, and even if I didn't know you, I have common sense. We are at a mall in one of the biggest cities in the world; you really want me to believe that in three hours, you couldn't find a single present for anyone? So which was it—the girls or the video games?" Michael said with a smile.

"Ha-ha. I was playing video games. They have some great games, and they even have this new football game that is so realistic. The graphics are amazing. It's really cool; you would probably like it since you're too old to play real football now," Christopher joked.

"Too old? Boy, I can still throw the ball better than you any day of the week! But seriously, when are you going to get your presents? You don't have to get me anything, but you should try to get something for your mom and brother. You know how your mother loves this time of year, and where's your Christmas cheer?"

Christopher answered quickly, "Who cares about cheer? Besides, Christmas is for kids Joey's age."

"What's that supposed to mean? You're too old for Christmas now?"

"Maybe I am," Christopher said matter-of-factly as only a teenager could have.

"Listen, Son, there is a lot more to Christmas than just Santa, presents, and cooking. It's a celebration of Jesus's birth as well as a time for miracles and hope. It's the time of year that can bring out the best in people. You know I'm not as religious as some, but I know that much," Michael said with care.

"Dad, look around here! What miracles do you see happening? I mean, all I see are parents fighting over the newest toy that's out for their kids. People compete to see who can give the most expensive gifts; they complain about waiting in lines; and then when it's over, they all complain about how they spent too much money and how it went by too fast. What's the miracle in that? What's so special about that?"

"Chris, you are only sixteen years old, and you are starting to sound like a cynical old man. Talk about seeing the glass as half empty. What happened to that positive attitude you always have? Miracles still happen every day, but most people don't take the time to recognize them. I'll tell you what. You want to see something special? Look at your mom and brother right now. Look at the awe and excitement on Joey's face as he's sitting on Santa's lap. Look at the smile on your mom's face as she's watching her son be happy. That is special, and those looks of pure joy are miracles."

"No, Dad, it's not a miracle. It's a lie. Like I said, Christmas is for kids Joey's age. They have all that joy now, and then they find out it was all a scam. As for Mom, well, Mom is just an exception," Christopher said.

"No, Son, your mom is exceptional! She's one of the few people who never forgot the true meaning of the holiday. Sure, she loves all the little-kid things that go with the season, but if you look at her heart, you can see the spirit of Christmas in her. You can see the spirit of unconditional love. That is what some say the true meaning of Christmas is: love. And your mom is one of the few people who remembers that all year long."

"Oh, come on, Dad. You're starting to sound like one of those people in the movies. This is the real world. The happiness that Mom has and shows has nothing to do with Christmas, God, Jesus, or any of that stuff. Mom is happy because she's a good person who has a good family and a good life. There's no other special reason why she's happy, and it has nothing to do with some higher power!" Christopher said.

Just then, Mary and Joey walked up. Michael and Christopher stood up to greet them.

"Daddy, Daddy, did you see me with Santa? I told him I've been a good boy all year, and he said that I'll get what I want for Christmas!" Joey said ecstatically.

"He said that, huh? Well, you must have really been good all year if he said that," Michael responded, smiling from ear to ear.

Christopher leaned over to his dad's ear and whispered, "You see, Dad? More lies to scare kids into behaving all year round. Just like the promise of a paradise like heaven to keep people in line."

"Okay, that's enough, Chris. We'll discuss this later!" Michael said sternly, slightly annoyed that Joey or Mary could have heard what they were talking about.

"What's going on?" Mary asked with a concerned look on her face.

"Nothing, Ma. We were just talking about the Bears and who they have to play this week," Christopher said quickly with half a smile.

"Oh, well, you can have that male-bonding stuff later. Right now, let's go home," Mary said with her contagious smile.

The family of four got into their car and started the long drive home. While the mall was only seven miles from their house, with the city traffic and a stop light on every block, it took them almost thirty-five minutes to arrive at their house. As soon as they got home, Christopher ran up the stairs of the two-story home, went into his bedroom, and changed his clothes. He had used the time during the car ride from the mall to text some of his friends from his cell phone to organize a game of pickup football. Some had agreed to meet at the neighborhood park, and they had enough people for a five-on-five game of tackle football. Shabbona Park was the perfect place for a bunch of boys to take out their teenage anger and frustration for a few hours by playing the greatest contact sport there was: football. It also helped that the park was located right in the center of all the streets where Christopher and his friends lived. Many friendships had been built on the grass of the beautiful park.

CHAPTER 2

Feelings

WHENEVER CHRISTOPHER PLAYED
football, his best friend, Johnny, was always there with him.
The two had been best friends since their first day of kindergarten,
and they always did everything together. Johnny wasn't the smartest
or most studious kid in the neighborhood, but he was loyal and was
a true friend to Christopher. There was nothing they wouldn't have
done for each other. They constantly watched each other's backs, and
the two were inseparable. In fact, Johnny had been at Christopher's
side in most of the fights he had been in. Whenever they had to fight
another group of kids, they almost always ended up victorious. Even
when the odds were against them and even if they lost the fight, they
always stood together against adversity.

One time in particular stood out to Christopher. An older kid in
the neighborhood had decided it was Johnny's turn to be the one who
got picked on. The boy, Luke, was about five years older than Johnny
and Christopher. There was a huge difference in strength and speed
between a fifteen-year-old teen and a ten-year-old boy. As Johnny
and Christopher were walking home, Luke came up behind them
and pushed them both on their backs, knocking them down to the

ground. Luke then picked up Johnny and demanded that he hand over any money he had in his pockets. Johnny, who was naturally stubborn, stood up to Luke and refused to give him a thing. The funny part was that Johnny only had a single dollar on him. But he would rather have taken a beating than give in and let Luke have that dollar.

Luke was angry at the defiance shown by the much smaller and weaker Johnny and decided to take out his anger on him the only way he knew how. Luke pulled his arm back to punch Johnny in the face. Luke believed that violence had to be the punishment for the defiance and the nonpayment. But just as Luke's arm was fully cocked back, Christopher came from behind to his friend's rescue and punched Luke in the back of the head. Even though Christopher was a good fighter for his age, the punch from the ten-year-old just angered Luke rather than knocking him down. Luke let go of his grip on Johnny and turned to come after Christopher for getting involved. Christopher kept backing up as Luke stomped toward him.

"Okay, you little punk! You want to protect your friend? Then I guess you can take the beat-down I was going to give him!" Luke shouted with fury. As with most bullies, Luke figured the louder he shouted the more scared his victims would be.

Christopher kept backing up from Luke, but he did not want to turn and run away, for he knew that the older and faster Luke would catch him. He did not want to turn his back and give Luke the opportunity to strike. At least while facing him, he felt he had a chance to defend himself.

Luke finally grabbed Christopher. Christopher punched Luke in the chin, but Luke just smiled. He pulled his arm back and prepared to show Christopher what a real punch to the chin should feel like. However, this time, when Luke's arm was pulled all the way back, Johnny came from behind and kicked Luke in the back of the knee as if he were kicking a soccer ball. Luke's leg buckled, and he let go of Christopher. Luke then turned back toward Johnny, who quickly retreated down the block. The situation then turned into a monkey-in-the-middle comedy for the three. Whenever Luke got close enough to grab one of the friends, the other would come to the rescue and strike Luke from the other side. The back-and-forth lasted all the way down the street, until finally, they were in front of Christopher's house, and the two friends were able to make a run for it. They managed to make it inside the house without Luke ever getting to enforce his beating.

The two friends would remember that episode forever. Luke never caught up with them that day or any day after that. It was a good lesson to them. Even though neither of them could have defeated the older boy on his own, by sticking together, as true friends did, they had survived the battle without being hurt or losing their money. The incident also cemented their friendship and proved that the two could count on each other no matter the obstacle. At any time, one of them could have run away and left the other to be beaten by Luke, but they had remained strong and stood side by side. That was what true friends were supposed to do, and needless to say, they always walked home together after that incident.

Finally, all the friends Christopher had texted arrived at the park, so they could play their game of football. The minute the last person got there, the game started. They picked players and split into two teams, and of course, Christopher had to be the quarterback of his team. He liked playing all positions, but quarterback was by far his favorite. To him, it was the position that had the most control and required the most thought. He thrived on taking the snap, seeing how the defense was going to play, and then making the quick decision to take advantage of them. He was good at it too. Christopher approached football the way others approached a game of chess. He always tried to anticipate the opponents' moves and stay two steps ahead of them. He loved the competition and strategy involved in the game. If they were going to blitz, he would buy time by scrambling and throw the ball deep to a receiver matched up one on one. If they played a deep coverage, he would take what the defense gave him and throw the ball short. Playing that position came easily to him, and he felt comfortable in doing it.

Coaches had always told Christopher he was too short to be a quarterback. That hadn't mattered when he played organized football when he was younger, but as he had gotten older, he had discovered the truth. Sadly, the coaches were right, which was why he had never tried out for the high school football teams. Christopher stood only five foot nine, but he had a strong build and was fast. His muscular legs gave him good balance, while his broad shoulders and upper-body strength made him hard to tackle. Of course, it didn't hurt that he and his father had spent countless hours watching Walter Payton highlight films while he was growing up. Christopher had learned to try to mimic Walter's juke moves to make defenders miss.

Christopher loved football more than all the other sports combined. Christopher was a good athlete in all sports, but he knew he wasn't exceptional at them. He knew he would never get a scholarship to college for playing, and it was certainly never going to be a career for him. But it didn't matter; he loved to play for the fun and competition of it. Sports were a great outlet for him and also a great way to be part of a team. Even if he wasn't on a school team, he had his team of friends at the park. Ironically, whenever Christopher had a chance to play against kids who did play on the school teams, he always came out victorious. One time, the high school's starting quarterback and his teammates had come out to play a pickup game against Christopher and his friends. The school team players had even worn their school jerseys, perhaps thinking that would intimidate their opponents. The strategy had not gone as hoped for the jersey-wearing jocks, as they'd left the game defeated after Christopher proved he was the far superior quarterback that day. Still, Christopher was never one to rub a defeat in an opponent's face. He actually had become friends with many of the school players that day, and some of them routinely played in the Shabbona Park pickup games.

After spending the first half of the day at the mall, Christopher was happy to finally be with his group of friends. They played all afternoon in the park, tackling each other in play after play in the snow. There were great plays, laughing, arguing, and hard hitting. It was everything a fun game among friends should have been. Finally, even though they wanted to play forever, it was time to end the contest. By that time, everyone was pretty worn out from expending so much energy as well as from the cold weather. Christopher's team had won, with Christopher throwing four touchdown passes and returning a kickoff for another. He was always one of the best athletes when they got together to play, and others always wanted Christopher on their team.

They all headed home, but Johnny decided to walk with Christopher back to his house to hang out for a while. As they walked, they talked about the game, including what they had done well and what they could have done better. Johnny wasn't nearly the all-around athlete Christopher was, but he was fast—probably the fastest out of all the friends in the neighborhood. That made him the perfect wide receiver for Christopher to throw the long ball to. In fact, two of the touchdowns Christopher had thrown that day had been to Johnny. They talked about those two touchdowns and how they could have had more. One of the touchdown passes had come on one of their favorite patterns to run: a deep post route. Johnny always had the speed to run fast down the sideline, and while the person covering him tried to keep up, he would turn diagonally and continue toward the center of the field to run the post. That gave Christopher the luxury of throwing the ball as far as he could down the center of the field and allowing Johnny, with his superior speed, to run under the ball for the catch. It was a thing of beauty to watch the spiraling football leave Christopher's hand, cutting through the cold, crisp winter air, and then land softly in Johnny's outstretched hands, hitting him in perfect stride.

They also discussed how much they loved being on the winning team and how great it was when they beat their other friends. Johnny was almost as competitive as Christopher, so he too thrived on the challenge of winning. Christopher loved the competition more, but Johnny loved the winning more. That was probably what led the two friends to have so many arguments over silly games, from video games to board games, such as Monopoly. There were many days when the Monopoly board flew across one of their bedrooms as the two friends played. When younger, they had argued a lot over such foolish games. The competitiveness the two shared was probably why they made such good teammates and why they always wanted to be on the same team.

They continued walking and talking about different subjects, taking their time and enjoying each other's company. Then Johnny asked a simple and innocent question. He could not have anticipated the emotional reaction he would receive. Johnny asked, "So did you get all your Christmas shopping done with your parents?"

Christopher gave him a look of disgust. Johnny was about to witness one of the greatest venting sessions he had ever seen in his lifetime. Christopher responded by letting go of everything he had been feeling.

"It was a big waste of time! It was a few hours of my life that I can never get back. Hours when I could have been sleeping or playing ball or something. I mean, all these people at the mall were waiting in line to see Santa, waiting in lines to buy things, fighting over parking spaces, and fighting over who was there first, and all for what? A silly holiday to make toy and greeting card companies rich.

A holiday based on someone who was probably just a very good man who had delusions of grandeur. I mean, if Jesus were really the Son of God, you'd think he would have known that if he went around announcing that to people, somebody would try to kill him or lock him up or something. If someone tried saying stuff like that today, they would put him in a mental institution!"

Johnny was in shock. He did not come from a very religious background, but even he was offended by what Christopher was saying. "Chris, how can you talk like that? Jesus died for us. Since when do you question that? And Christmas is the celebration of his birth. What's not to be happy about?"

"Johnny, I don't expect you to understand or agree with me, but I'm just looking at the facts. When I was studying for my confirmation, we even talked about how people who grew up in the same town as Jesus didn't believe he was the Son of God. He was a carpenter. A very nice, possibly educated, and compassionate carpenter, but he was still just a carpenter."

"You need to calm down, man. Talking that junk isn't good, bro. It's evil. Plus, I don't want to be standing next to you when a lightning bolt comes down on you. Tell me this: If he was just a carpenter, how come people still celebrate him and his works all around the world more than two thousand years after he died? I can't even remember my own grandmother's birthday, and she's still alive!"

"Man, they remember because they are taught to remember. Look at all the companies that make money off Christmas and Easter. They sell toys, cards, chocolates, and whatever else, but it's all a scam. Jesus was not the Son of God, even if there is one!" Christopher said.

"Wow, seriously, man? Now you are saying that God isn't real either. You've got serious issues. Where is all this coming from? I've known you our whole lives and never heard you talk like this."

"Think about it, bro. Scientists can now explain most of the supposed miracles in the Bible by what we know through technology and stuff. The people who wrote the Bible had no way of understanding the stuff we know about now—things like weather, natural disasters, medicine, and whatever else. They also didn't have cops, the FBI, the CIA, courtrooms, lawyers, and all that junk. So the only way to keep people from committing crimes all the time was to threaten them. They needed a threat to keep them in line. What threat did they use? The threat of a higher being who can send you to an eternal place of torture if you don't do the right things. But it was all a lie, just like Christmas is!" Christopher finally took a breath after spilling all of his feelings.

"Chris, like I said, I've never heard you talk like this. And to be honest with you, I don't like it. You know I'm not Mr. Holy Roller or anything, but even I know that what you are saying is disrespectful. Hopefully you are just having a bad day and don't really feel this way. I don't think I've ever seen you this negative and down on something. It's not you, bro. Anyway, this conversation is gettin' way too deep for me; I'm gonna head on home now to take a shower. I'll talk to you later when you've calmed down a little bit." With that, Johnny turned and started to walk home.

"Johnny, wait, man! My bad. I didn't mean to sound like I was yellin' at you or to upset you, man. I've just been frustrated by this, and today I reached my boiling point. I just don't understand why people don't see things like I do."

"Whatever, Chris. We're cool. I'm still gonna head home, though. You sound like you may need some alone time anyway. Do me a favor, though, would ya? Don't let your mom hear you talkin' that crazy stuff. It'll really hurt her. You know she's sensitive. Good game, though, man. I'll talk to ya later!" Johnny turned to walk away.

"Yeah, man, good game. All right, I'll hit ya up later," Christopher replied, feeling a little bad about unloading all of his frustrations on his friend, who had just asked how his morning had gone, trying to be nice. He also knew that Johnny was right about not letting his mom hear him talk that way. It would have broken her heart, as she would have felt it was somehow her fault that he felt that way.

"See? There's another problem with religions! Guilt! My mom would feel guilty because I don't believe what she believes, and she would feel responsible," he said to himself. Christopher never wanted his mom to feel that way, but he did feel that she was misguided when it came to God.

He turned around to go into his house and was shocked to see his dad standing on the porch. "How long have you been standing there, Dad?" Christopher asked.

"For a few minutes now. You know, just long enough to hear that now you don't believe in God anymore. Do you really feel that way deep down, or are you just looking for answers?" Michael asked.

"I'm sorry you had to hear that, Dad, but I really don't want to talk about this with you right now."

"But you want to talk about it with Johnny? Why do you think you can make him understand how you feel easier than you can make me understand?"

"I just know how you feel, and I don't want to upset you. You are sensitive enough at this time of year anyway."

"Well, thank you, but you're not the only person to have ever had these doubts about God. Many people question their faith, Son, but that's why it's called faith. There are some things we can't prove; we just have to believe in them."

"Why? Why on this one subject are we supposed to just blindly believe something, when we know that everything else in life we should question? And since you really want me to talk to you about this, let me ask you another thing. Why, out of all the planets in the universe, would an all-powerful and all-knowing God choose to send his Son to this planet? I mean, back then, people thought Earth was the only planet, and even after they discovered the other planets, they still believed our planet was the only one to have life on it. Now we know that there are billions of planets out there. There is a good possibility life exists on some other planets out there in the universe. So why would the Son of God choose this one planet to come to? Especially since all the people and customs were so barbaric back then?"

"I don't know, Son; I'm not God. But let me tell you this. There is a movie that was made a long time ago called *The Song of Bernadette.* There is a line in that movie that I will never forget, and you're reminding me of it right now."

"What's that?" Christopher asked sarcastically.

"'For those who don't believe, no explanation is possible. For those who do believe, no explanation is necessary.'"

"How in the world does that remind you of me?" Christopher asked.

"Because of the way you are talking and feeling right now. I think that if Jesus himself came down to talk to you, you probably still wouldn't believe him."

"Well, Dad, maybe if something like that happened, I would believe, but that would be a miracle. Like I said earlier at the mall, miracles don't happen anymore!"

Michael turned to go inside, shaking his head in disbelief. He was shocked at how Christopher was thinking. *What happened to make my son feel this way?* he wondered. Christopher had always been such a positive person, and it was strange for him to be so stubbornly negative and skeptical on the issue. His grandmother's passing had had an effect on him and maybe had shaken his faith. Christopher had seen a lot of trying and confusing things in his life already at a young age. In the past five years, he had seen a lot of loss, as was common in the big city. In addition to his grandmother's death, he had lost a friend who died in a car accident, another friend had gone to jail for drugs, one of his classmates had died of an overdose, and another close friend's father had died of cancer. In addition, most of his cousins and family he was close with had moved away. They tried to keep in touch, but with the exception of the occasional phone call or text message, contact with them was not like it used to be. At sixteen years old, he was already dealing with loss in many ways.

Michael then thought that maybe it was a miracle Christopher was as positive and upbeat as he was. Perhaps that was a testament to his strength and character, and maybe those trials would lead him to have a stronger sense of faith rather than lose it altogether. Michael began to pray as he walked away, asking God not to give up on his son and to always keep him safe.

Christopher sat outside on the porch in the cold for a few minutes longer after his dad went inside. He just wanted to sit there in the winter air with his thoughts. He thought about how smart his father was, and he wondered why his dad couldn't see the possibility that the truth was completely different from what they had been led to believe in churches. How could someone of his dad's intelligence level believe something to be true based solely on faith and without any factual evidence to back it? The more Christopher thought about it, the angrier he became and the more he convinced himself that his way of thinking was the correct way. He convinced himself that his way of thinking was the only way to think. Negativity had a way of doing that to people. The more negative and angry they became the more they stopped looking for answers and were content with thinking everyone else was wrong. Of course, no one ever would have admitted he or she was negative, and Christopher didn't see himself as being that way either. In his mind, he was correct, and he had the facts to back it up.

Christopher looked up as he heard his neighbor across the street shout to him, "Merry Christmas!" Christopher tried with all his might not to roll his eyes at the neighbor or, worse, tell him to shut up. He did the polite thing: he just smiled and waved back at him.

When he was ready to go inside, he walked through the front door, and to his left was the Christmas tree, all colorfully lit up and beautifully decorated. Then he turned to his right and saw a miniature manger set up on the table, with baby Jesus right in the middle, looking up at him. Christopher then turned back to the left and saw more Christmas decorations hanging all around the house. He had always loved the way his mother went all out in decorating the whole house and filling it with holiday cheer, but at that minute, he could not bring himself to appreciate all the hard work she had put in to decorating. He just rolled his eyes and walked up the stairs.

He reached the top of the staircase, went to his bedroom, and looked over toward his desk in the corner of the room. He noticed the cross that was always sitting on his desk. His parents had given it to him as a present after he made his confirmation. It was a beautiful crystal cross about a foot tall and about six inches wide at the base. An engraved inscription on the base read, "For God so loved the world that he gave his only begotten son." Christopher looked at it, shook his head with a sarcastic smirk, and then picked up the cross and put it in his desk drawer so it was out of sight. He was not in the mood to see a cross. The strong faith he had had after his confirmation was in danger of being lost forever.

He got out of his dirty, sweaty football clothes and went to take a shower, as he normally did after playing. He thought maybe taking a shower would calm him down and allow him to think about other things. After he finished cleaning up and got dressed, he went downstairs to eat dinner with his family.

Mary had made chicken parmesan over rigatoni noodles, one of Christopher's favorite dishes. He could smell the wonderful aroma of it as he walked down the stairs, and it made his mouth water with anticipation. He couldn't wait to sink his teeth into the perfectly breaded chicken breast smothered with marinara sauce and layers of mozzarella cheese. He had worked up quite an appetite and burned a lot of calories while running around in the snow earlier. It was the perfect meal to put him in a better mood.

Every night, the family ate dinner together in front of the television. They would all watch a movie or one of their favorite television shows, depending on what day of the week it was, and that night was no different. They always took turns picking out movies to watch. That night was Joey's turn to pick the movie, and Christopher laughed at the thought of what Joey might pick. Would he perhaps pick a superhero movie to watch? Or maybe he would select a cartoon of some sort. It didn't matter what Joey picked; it was fun for Christopher to see how happy Joey got when announcing his selection. He was always so proud of himself, which made his big brother smile with pride.

Joey and Christopher had a special bond, as many brothers did. Some might have thought the large difference in their ages, ten years, was a detriment to their relationship, but it never was that way to them. Christopher always looked at Joey as a miniature version of himself, and he was old enough to be a role model instead of being a competitor, as some siblings closer in age were. Joey always looked at Christopher with nothing but admiration. Though Christopher was older than he was, Christopher always made time for him and made him feel special. For example, every day when Christopher got home from school, he would take Joey out into the backyard to play catch or a short game of Wiffle ball with him. Even if it was only for a half hour before Christopher went to do something with his friends, he always made time for Joey. Sure, they fought sometimes, as brothers did, but Joey told all his friends at school that he had the best big brother in the world. It was a title Christopher enjoyed and wanted to keep.

The family all sat down to eat the delicious chicken parmesan dinner, and Christopher asked, "So what are we watchin' with dinner?" He couldn't wait to hear Joey yell out what he had selected.

"*The Grinch!*" Joey shouted happily with the sense of accomplishment Christopher loved. Unfortunately, the choice couldn't have come at a less opportune time.

"Can't we watch something else?" Christopher asked his little brother.

"No, Chris, your brother wants to watch that. It's his turn to pick a movie, and plus, it is a Christmas movie. Besides, you've been acting like a Grinch today, so it might do you some good to watch it," Mary replied with her infectious smile, trying to make both a joke and a point.

"Oh, come on, Ma. Can't we watch—"

"No, Christopher, you heard your mother. Joey chose this movie to watch with his turn. We are watching this, and it's not up for debate," Michael said in his fatherly tone of voice.

"Yay!" Joey yelled with glee. He loved the Grinch movie and had been looking forward to it all day.

Christopher finally gave in and started eating the dinner his mother had prepared. He ate quickly. The meal he had been looking forward to had somehow lost its appeal. He couldn't enjoy the chicken parmesan he loved, because it seemed that with each minute the movie played, he became more agitated. He couldn't seem to shovel the food into his mouth fast enough. He finally finished his plate and got up to go to his room.

"Where are you going, sweetie? Don't you want a second plate?" Mary asked.

"No, thanks, Ma. I'm full. It was very good."

"You're full? Off of one plate? Are you feeling okay?"

"Yeah, Ma, I'm fine. I think I just ran so much today that I actually lost my appetite."

"Well, don't you want to at least finish watching the movie with us?" she asked.

"Not really. I've seen it a hundred times. I'm going to go play my PlayStation or something. Don't worry, though. I'm fine," he said.

Christopher turned to walk up the stairs, and Mary looked at her husband with an expression that seemed to shout, "What's wrong with our son?" Michael just shook his head and shrugged as if to say he didn't know.

"Look, Mommy, it's the Grinch!" Joey shouted while looking at the movie, oblivious to the conversation going on around him.

"Yes, honey, it sure is," Mary responded as she watched Christopher walk up the stairs to his room.

Christopher walked into his bedroom, not knowing quite what to do with himself. It was too early to go to bed, nothing was on television except for Christmas specials, and he was not in the mood to play video games. He picked up his cell phone and thought about texting some of his friends to see if anyone wanted to get together to hang out, but he realized he didn't really want to see or talk to anyone either. He was annoyed at all of the day's events aside from the football game they had played. He then joked to himself that it could have been worse—he could have lost the game.

He lazily plopped down onto his bed and looked up at the ceiling. He let his eyes aimlessly wander around the room until they made their way to the wall displaying pictures of Chicago sports legends. Framed pictures of Michael Jordan, Walter Payton, Scottie Pippen, and other legends hung on the wall. The people of Chicago loved their sports heroes. When the Bulls, the Bears, the Blackhawks, or one of the baseball teams was winning, it was as if the whole city came together for a while. It didn't matter what ethnicity, religion, or political affiliation they belonged to, when it came to their sports, they were all united as Chicagoans rooting for their teams. The outcome of a single Bears game could make the difference between a good week and a bad week. Many people in the city, like Christopher and his dad, lived vicariously through their sports teams. They felt the pain of losing and the joy of winning games probably more than the athletes they were watching.

Christopher got up and shuffled over to his window to look out at the city he loved so much. He looked out at the skyline of towering skyscrapers that stood against the backdrop of the night sky. Then he looked up at the beautiful twinkling stars, and he wondered, *How many civilizations are out there that we don't know about?* Were they friendly? Were they vicious? Were they intelligent? Were they warrior-like? Were they more advanced or less advanced than humans? As those thoughts ran through his head, he turned to walk back to his bed and noticed that his crystal cross was back on his desk. "I know I put that in the drawer," he said to himself. *Mom must have come in here when I was in the shower and put it back*, he thought.

Once again, he picked it up; shook his head at it, almost in disgust; and put it in the drawer. He lay back down on the bed, picked up the remote control, and turned on the TV. He searched for anything worth watching that was not some type of Christmas special. He had gone through almost every channel, when finally he came across an NBA basketball game. He remembered with excitement that the Chicago Bulls were playing, and he couldn't believe he had been so aggravated that he had forgotten the game was on. Basketball was Christopher's second-favorite sport, and he enjoyed playing that as well. Of course, in Chicago, he had to find an indoor court to play on for most months of the year. He had loved watching and rooting for the Bulls since the days of Michael Jordan, just like every other person in the city of Chicago or any person who loved basketball. His vast collection of Jordan sneakers in the closet was another sign of his admiration of the greatest basketball player to ever step onto the court.

He sat up intently to watch, as the game was tight. It was the third quarter, and the teams were trading baskets back and forth. Both teams were playing well offensively, hitting three-pointers and pushing the fast breaks when available. It was a great game, with the lead going back and forth. Christopher was so engrossed in the game that he forgot all about Christmas and why he had been so upset earlier. Before he knew it, only thirty-seven seconds were left in the game, and the Bulls were trailing by two points. The other team had the ball, and they made a fifteen-foot jump shot to go up by four points with only eighteen seconds left.

"No, don't give them an open shot like that!" Christopher shouted at the television, as if the players could somehow hear him. The Bulls' star player took the ball down the court and pulled up at the three-point line. He jumped, flicked his wrist, and released the ball with perfect follow-through; the ball arced through the air and swished through the bottom of the net. The Bulls were now down by one point with ten seconds left. The same player suddenly stole the ball from the other team on the inbounds pass and dribbled the ball out to the top of the key. As the clock counted down—seven seconds, six seconds, five seconds—he dribbled to the right. Four seconds, three seconds—he pulled up from sixteen feet and shot. Two seconds, one second—the ball went through the net. The Bulls won!

"Yes! Wow! What a shot! I can't believe it! Amazing! Yes, yes, yes! What an ending!" Christopher shouted with joy. Some sports fans got so worked up and into their teams' games that it was as if they too had been on the court participating or, even better, their cheering for the team somehow had had a magical effect on the outcome.

The team on the court went crazy with excitement at winning, jumping and hugging their star, almost tackling him to the ground in their joy. Only when the television crew came up for an interview was the hero of the game able to get away. "What a way to end the game," the reporter said. "You came down the court trailing by four, hit a three-point shot, stole the inbound pass, and then hit the game-winning jumper at the buzzer. What were you thinking when you were down by four with only eighteen seconds left?"

"Well, I was thinking that there was still enough time for us to win, but we needed to execute. I came down the court and made the three to cut it to a one-point lead. Then I was like, *Okay, we need to get the ball back.* I was able to get the steal, and then by the grace of God, my shot went in at the buzzer, and we won. What can I say? It's the season of miracles, right?" he said with a genuine smile.

Christopher's expression of joy and excitement turned into a look of shock as his eyes widened in anger. "By the grace of God?" he said. "You made the shot, you idiot, not God! What did God have to do with it? What is wrong with all these people? I can't even watch a game without hearing about God. There is no God! And if there were, he wouldn't care about basketball; he would care about ending wars, curing cancer, and stopping innocent kids from dying on the street. These people are all brainwashed." Christopher grabbed the remote control and turned the power to the television off in disgust. He sat there on his bed, shaking his head, thinking about how he had gone from being happy to being aggravated again. He stood up to walk out of the room and threw the remote control across the room onto the bed. He decided to go downstairs to get something to drink. He hoped he could relax a little bit and calm down.

Michael asked, "Hey, Chris, do you know if the Bulls won or not?"

After rolling his eyes to himself, Christopher answered, "Yeah, the Bulls won. Apparently, God hit a shot to win the game at the buzzer."

"What?" Michael asked, thinking his hearing was going. "Who hit a shot at the buzzer?"

"The Bulls did. They were losing by four but came back in the last minute and won by a point," Christopher said to avoid getting even more upset.

Christopher walked back upstairs to his room with his drink in hand. He shut the door behind him and lay down on his bed again. Christopher's bedroom was the only one on the second floor. His parents' and Joey's bedrooms were on the first floor, which worked out well to give the teenager of the house a little bit of privacy. He needed it that day because everything seemed to be aggravating him, he thought. Christopher was just starting to relax, when his mom called up to him from downstairs.

"Christopher, we're all going to bed! Can you come down here to take the trash out real quick?" Mary asked.

"Now, Ma? Can't I do it in the morning?" Christopher said.

"Please do it now, honey. The garbage stinks, and you know you'll sleep in until the football pregame shows start."

"Fine, I'll come do it now," Christopher said reluctantly.

Christopher grabbed his jacket and walked back downstairs. He went into the kitchen, picked up the bag of garbage and the recycling, and walked outside into the night cold. It was so windy that the bag of trash almost flew out of his hands while he walked down the gateway to the trash cans. He put the bag into the large metal garbage can in the alley and then looked down the alleyway. He just stood there for a minute, staring and listening to the sounds of the city. It was always awake; some activity was always going on. He could hear faint sounds of traffic and sirens in the distance. He felt comfort in hearing the sounds of the city, and standing there in the cold, he began to finally calm down. What some considered noise he found soothing. He remembered that no matter how aggravated he was, there were a lot of people out there much worse off than he was. After a few minutes, he went back inside into the nice, cozy comfort of the warm house.

"Thank you, Chris!" Mary yelled out from her bedroom as he walked in from the cold.

"You're welcome, Ma!" Christopher shouted back as he walked back up the stairs to his room to begin getting ready for bed.

CHAPTER 3

The Journey Begins

CHRISTOPHER WALKED INTO HIS ROOM and took his gold chain from around his neck. He placed it on his dresser and then took off his jacket and threw it onto the bed. He was about to take his sneakers off before going into the bathroom to brush his teeth, but he again saw his crystal cross back on the desk. He was not only confused but also slightly annoyed as he stood there trying to figure out how the cross, which he had put away twice, had made its way back onto the desk.

"What did Mom do—sneak back in here when she made me take out the trash?" Christopher asked himself. He had just calmed down again, and in what seemed like a never-ending cycle that night, he again became upset at the sight of the cross and what it represented. He angrily walked over to the desk and picked the cross up to put it back in the drawer once and for all. He opened the drawer and found a gift box lying in the drawer. "This wasn't here before," he said to himself, confused. He put the cross down on the desk and examined the mysterious gift.

The box was about the size of a box that a baseball would have fit into. There was a note attached to it: "To Christopher. From Michael.

Open immediately." Christopher wondered what his dad was up to. *Why would he sneak in here and give me a gift now? Why would he tell me to open it immediately? And why did he sign it as Michael instead of Dad? Oh, maybe it's a joke or something. Knowing Dad, it's probably a bad joke too.* Christopher laughed to himself.

He opened the box, and all of a sudden, a light came out of it. It was so bright and intense that it was as if all the rays of the sun had been inside the box and suddenly released. Christopher dropped the box to the floor, but it continued to radiate beams of light. He couldn't even look at it, as the light was blinding. He turned his head to try to cover his eyes, and then the entire room started to spin.

"What is going on?" Christopher yelled in fear.

The room spun faster and faster, and then he felt himself lifting off the ground as if he were floating. His legs rose as if a tornado were sucking him into its funnel. He realized the little box was causing this—he was somehow being pulled into the light-giving box. The force pulling him into the box gained strength. He was being sucked into it with great speed.

Christopher grabbed frantically for something—anything—to hold on to. He reached for his chair, but he could not get a grip. The force of the box pulled even stronger and sucked him in a little bit farther. The room spun even faster than before, making it almost impossible for Christopher to see what he was grabbing at. He was able to grab on to the desk, and he tried to pull himself out using all his strength. He was no match, however, for the power coming from the little gift, and he lost his grip once again.

His legs were now completely inside the tiny box. Panicking, he reached for anything, trying to get one last chance to pull himself out. It was all happening so fast. While it seemed to him that he had been fighting the force for a few minutes, it had really only been a few seconds. He made one last attempt to reach for his desk to escape the invisible force.

When he reached for the desk, he grabbed hold of the crystal cross he had been putting in the drawer all night long. He got one hand around it and then both hands, and then, all of a sudden, the cross started to glow as well. It glowed with a bright light that matched the intensity of the light coming from the box. Then, in the blink of an eye, Christopher and the crystal cross were both swallowed into the mysterious box.

The box stopped producing light and closed quietly after devouring them. The room stopped spinning. Christopher was no longer there.

Christopher found himself standing in the middle of an infinite darkness. The powerful whirlwind of the past few seconds was gone, along with the intense light that had accompanied it. He had no idea where he was, and he tried desperately to focus his eyes on something, but to no avail. There were none of the city sounds he had heard earlier in the alley, yet he believed he was outside, because he felt as if he were standing on grass. Still, he couldn't be sure where he was; it was too dark and too quiet to know anything. He knew only that he was no longer in his bedroom—or even in his house, for that matter. He knelt down to try to touch the ground. He was in fact standing on grass. It was different from the grass in front of his house, though, as it was level and cut short. There was no snow on the ground, which he found strange since it had been snowing almost all day. Even stranger, he had no jacket or sweatshirt on, but he wasn't cold.

Just then, Christopher heard a strange voice come out of the quiet darkness. "I heard you like the game of football," the mysterious, deep voice said.

"Who's that? Where am I?" Christopher asked, frightened.

"You mean you don't know?" the voice said.

"How could I? I can't see a thing!" Christopher said.

"That's interesting. You have to see something to believe it, do you? Well then, do you know where you are now?" the voice said.

Suddenly, lights came on all around Christopher. They were

stadium lights, and they came on one section at a time, forming a circle all around him. Christopher struggled to adjust his eyes after going from total darkness into the bright light. He looked around after blinking feverishly to try to focus and realized he was standing in a large football stadium. It was huge; it had navy and orange seats throughout and looked as if it could have held at least sixty thousand people. He looked down at his feet and saw that he was standing on a large orange *C* painted in the middle of the perfectly manicured green grass field. Christopher now knew exactly where he was. He was at historic Soldier Field, where his hometown Chicago Bears played their NFL home football games.

"Do you know where you are now?" the voice said.

"I'm in Soldier Field," Christopher said, confused.

"Are you sure?"

"Yes, I'm sure. I've watched the Bears play every Sunday since I was four years old. I still don't have a clue who you are, though." Christopher was frightened, annoyed, relaxed, and calm all at the same time. He knew that something strange had happened to bring him from his bedroom to the stadium. He knew he should have been freezing, but he wasn't. He knew he was talking to a voice, but he didn't know whom the voice belonged to or where it was coming from. He also knew he should have been afraid, but for some weird, unexplainable reason, he wasn't. The longer he was there, the calmer and more at peace he became.

"My name is Michael. I am the one who put the gift box in your room that proceeded to bring you here. It's kind of funny, isn't it?" the voice said.

"What's funny?" Christopher asked, trying to understand.

"Out of all the things you could have grabbed hold of when you were being pulled into the box, you chose to grab ahold of that," the voice said.

Christopher looked down to see what Michael was referring to and realized he was still holding the crystal cross in his hand. He looked at it in awe, as he hadn't even realized it had made the trip with him.

"People often reach out to him in times of desperation and fear," Michael said.

Christopher didn't even have time to process what Michael had just said. He put the crystal cross down on the crisp grass and kept looking around to try to find out where the voice was coming from. A thousand questions ran through his head, and he wanted the answers to all of them right now. He began to ask the questions all at once. "Why did you bring me here? How did you get into my room? What was that box? Why—"

"Whoa, kid, slow down," the mysterious Michael said. "I know you have a lot of questions, and we'll hopefully get to them all. But before that, since we are standing in this legendary stadium, let's throw the football around."

"Throw the football around? You have got to be kidding me. I have no idea who you are, and I still can't even see you! Where are you?"

"Turn around."

Christopher turned around quickly and saw nothing. "Where? I still don't see you!"

"Oh, that's right; I forgot. If you can't see me, you don't believe I'm here, right? Well, how about now?"

Just then, this Michael appeared right in front of Christopher's eyes. Christopher was so startled at the sudden appearance of the stranger that he had to take a few steps back and nearly lost his balance, almost falling to the ground. Christopher was now face-to-face with the source of the mysterious voice. Michael stood more than six feet tall and had a muscular, athletic build. He had short dark brown hair combed neatly straight back and piercing blue eyes that had a genuine warmth to them. He wore a pair of baggy blue jeans, sneakers, and a Walter Payton jersey.

"How did you appear out of nowhere like that?" Christopher asked.

"Are we going to throw the ball around or not?" Michael responded as he trotted about fifteen yards away from Christopher.

A football appeared in Michael's hand, and he wound up and threw it to Christopher. The young man was in shock when a magical ball appeared out of thin air and started flying toward him. He barely had time to raise his hands and dropped the ball after it hit him right in the stomach.

"That's not how you catch a ball, kid! I thought you played this game," Michael joked with a smile.

"Mister, how did you make that ball—"

"I told you: the name is Michael. But you can call me Mike if you want to. Now, are you going to throw the ball back to me or what, Mr. Quarterback?" Mike said.

"I must be dreaming. How did you know that I like to play quarterback?" Christopher asked.

"Again with the questions? Look, kid, I know a lot about you. That's my job. Now, would you please throw the ball back so I can see that arm of yours? I told you that we will get to all of your questions later. For now, just stop thinking, and throw the ball."

Christopher figured he should do what Michael had asked him to: throw the football. Mike had said he would answer all of Christopher's questions later, so there seemed to be no harm in playing a game of catch. Besides, part of him believed he was somehow in bed, dreaming all of this.

Christopher bent down to pick the ball up, but his hand went right through the ball. He tried again with the same result: his hand passed right through it. It was as if the football were just a mirage or a hologram or something. He tried a third time to pick it up, and again, the outcome was the same.

"What's the problem, kid? Can't you pick up a ball?" Mike asked.

"You see my hand going right through it, don't you? This ball isn't real!" Christopher said, slightly annoyed, as he didn't like being toyed with.

"But I don't understand. You can see it, and you said earlier that seeing is believing. If you can see it, then it is real, so you should be able to pick it up," said Mike.

"Very funny, but you saw me try to pick it up, and I couldn't. So it's not real."

"Okay, that's fair. So now you have to feel something to believe it is real. Okay, why don't you try to pick it up now?" Mike said.

"Fine!" Christopher rolled his eyes. He bent down to pick up the ball and was able to grab it that time, just as Mike had suggested. He didn't understand why he had been unable to pick up the ball before, but he had it now, so he drew his arm back to throw the ball.

Mike yelled, "Wait a minute! Where's the ball, Christopher?"

"What do you mean, bro? It's right here." Christopher looked at his hand in disbelief. He felt the ball in his hand—he had his fingers around the laces—but he could no longer see the ball. "What the ..." Christopher racked his brain, trying to figure out what was going on.

"It's okay. You feel it, don't you? So just throw the ball," Mike said.

"But I can't even see it!" Christopher shouted.

"Make up your mind, would you, kid? You just changed your mind from 'Seeing is believing' to 'Feeling is believing.' Now you want to change it back again? You feel it in your hand, so just throw it. You don't need to see it too," Mike said.

Christopher was fully convinced he was dreaming at that point. He had teleported from his room to Soldier Field and was talking to a stranger who could appear out of nowhere and do magic tricks with a football. He was either dreaming or completely losing his mind.

"Come on, Chris. We don't have all night to just stand here, you know."

As requested, Christopher threw the ball, even though he could not see it. As soon as it left his hand, the ball magically appeared again, darting through the air on a line and right into Mike's hands.

"Nice spiral, kid. You do have a decent arm."

"How did … What just … Did I …"

"Exactly. Come on now. Catch it," Mike said as he threw it back to him.

Christopher did not know what to make of everything that was happening. He still did not know who Michael was or what he wanted. He seriously doubted Mike had gone through so much trouble just to play catch with a disappearing football. However, Christopher was having fun all of a sudden. Unexplainably, he felt a feeling of joy come over him as he threw the football around with the stranger.

Christopher had never met Mike before, but somehow, he felt as if he had known him his whole life. The two of them took turns running different route patterns and throwing the ball to each other. Mike could throw the ball every bit as well as Christopher could; in fact, he threw it better than anyone Christopher had ever seen.

They laughed and ran the different routes, and Mike even made a couple diving catches to increase the level of excitement. Christopher never had thought he would have a chance to throw a football on that majestic field. He reveled in the moment, taking the time to enjoy the once-in-a-lifetime experience. Even if that wasn't the way he always had envisioned being on that field, the opportunity was there, and he was happy and grateful for it.

Mike then put the ball down and said, "That was fun. You're a decent quarterback, but more importantly, I can tell how much you love to play the game. You have a lot of passion for it. Tell me—what do you say when people tell you that football is stupid?"

"That's a strange question. I would say that they don't understand the game and don't love it like I do. They probably never gave it a chance. It takes time to understand the whole game and what's going on. I've been watching for twelve years and playing for ten, and I still don't know half as much as my dad does," Christopher responded, as if he had been asked that question before.

"That's interesting. So you think people sometimes judge things before they take the time to understand them completely—before they can develop a passion for them. I like that answer. Make sure you remember it later on. Right now, we have to go."

"Go? What do you mean *go*? Go where? I'm not going anywhere else with you. No offense, Mike, but I don't know you. I still don't know how or why you brought me here, and you haven't told me a single thing yet. You didn't even tell me how you did that trick with the ball," Christopher said.

"Trick? That was no trick, Chris. If you're talking about how the ball appeared and then disappeared, I had nothing to do with that. You made that happen!" Mike replied.

"What do you mean I made that happen?" Christopher asked sarcastically.

"Just what I said: you made it happen. You kept changing your perception of what *real* is. First, seeing something made it real to you, and then you decided that something real had to be something you could feel. You don't necessarily have to see something or touch something for it to be real. This was just a little exercise to make you aware of that. Now, let's go; we have a lot to see. No pun intended." Mike smiled.

"You promised to answer some of my questions. Can't you tell me who you are and why you brought me here before you expect me to go somewhere with you?"

"Fair enough. Just think of me as a friend, and the reason I brought you here is because you have some serious questions and concerns. I'm going to try to give you a chance to find the answers. What I just talked to you about was lesson number one. Let's move on to lesson number two," Mike said.

As quickly as he had appeared, Mike disappeared right in front of Christopher's eyes. With his disappearance, all the lights in the stadium shut off at the same time, and Christopher was again left alone, standing in the darkness. He spun around, trying to refocus his eyes on something—anything—but he was in pure darkness, as he had been before.

"Mike? Wait, Mike!" Christopher yelled out.

Mike's pure and deep voice then echoed throughout the darkness-filled stadium. "It's kind of a lonely feeling, standing there alone in the dark, isn't it? Lucky for you, there is always some light, even in complete darkness, if you know where to look."

"But I don't see any light at all," Christopher said.

Just then, he saw the crystal cross from his desk sitting in the grass right where he had put it down. All of a sudden, the cross began to glow. A beautiful, radiant, peaceful light shone from the cross, and Christopher felt drawn to it. He walked over and knelt down beside the beautifully illuminated cross. It seemed to be calling out to him. Christopher wrapped his hand around the base of the cross. He felt a warm, loving sensation go through his body, passing through one cell at a time, the way a set of dominos fell one at a time, with each touching the next. Mike's voice then seemed to whisper in Christopher's ear: "He is the way, the truth, the light."

All of a sudden, Christopher felt everything start to spin around him again. He instinctively clutched on to the cross as tightly as he could. The light of the cross grew even brighter, and then the cross shot up into the sky, bringing Christopher along for a ride. It pulled him upward into the night sky, and he had no control over where he was going or in which direction. Before he knew it, he was above the stadium, looking down on it. Then he was high above the city. The lights and buildings were beautiful from that angle.

The towering skyscrapers of the skyline got smaller and smaller as Christopher was pulled higher and higher. Soon he could see nothing except the clouds below him. Next, he was pulled outside Earth's atmosphere, and he looked down on the beautiful blue planet. There were no words to express what he was seeing. He was too amazed to say anything as he tried to take in as much of the fantastic ride as possible. He moved faster and faster as the cross pulled him past the moon. Earth now looked like a tiny blue marble. The speed at which he was traveling increased even more. He flew past all the planets. He passed the Red Planet, Mars. Next, he passed the enormous Jupiter and all of its moons. He passed the amazing rings of Saturn and then Uranus, Neptune, and Pluto. Each heavenly body passed by quicker than the previous one. Then the logical part of Christopher's mind kicked in.

"Mike, how am I breathing in space? There's no oxygen out here!" he said, hoping Mike could hear him.

"Relax, kid. Just enjoy the ride," Mike said.

Christopher knew that was exactly what he should do. Why was he even trying to make any sense of what was happening to him that night? He couldn't have explained any of it even if he had tried, so why wonder about things he obviously couldn't control? Yes, logically, he knew he shouldn't have been able to breathe in space. But logically, he shouldn't have been able to fit into a tiny gift box or be teleported instantaneously from his bedroom to a football stadium either. As Mike had suggested, he would just try to enjoy the ride and take in all of the breathtaking sights. He was now completely outside Earth's solar system. With his speed still increasing, he passed through the entire Milky Way Galaxy in no more than a few seconds. He was able to focus for a minute on the spiral-shaped galaxy, which he had seen many pictures of in school. *Those pictures sure didn't do the real thing justice*, he thought to himself. He thought he must have been at top speed now, because stars and planets were flying past him so fast that he felt as if he were in a *Star Wars* movie. The stars seemed to be long rows of lights that were all connected somehow.

After a few more minutes of high-speed travel, the cross all of a sudden stopped glowing, and Christopher came to a sudden halt. He hovered there in space, floating like a buoy in the ocean.

"I wonder where I am," he said.

He looked down below his dangling Nike sneakers, and right below him was a humongous planet that looked as if it could have fit five planet Earths inside it. It was a color he had never seen before—a combination of purples, blues, yellows, and grays. The colors seemed more vibrant than the colors of Earth.

"What is this planet below me? Mike, why am I stopped here?" Christopher asked.

Mike did not answer, but the crystal cross lit up again. The cross pulled him down into the beautifully colored planet. It pulled him through the planet's atmosphere so fast that a white glow surrounded him like a cocoon. The glow was so bright and intense that it was all Christopher could see around him. He knew he was traveling at an extremely fast rate of speed. Suddenly, the white glow around him vanished. The light of the cross extinguished, and incredibly, Christopher found he had safely landed feet first on the strange new planet.

The young man looked around, trying to comprehend the last few minutes of his life. It was not every day that a human being traveled at the speed of light from one galaxy to the next, let alone found himself standing on a strange new planet. It seemed even more unlikely considering that the object that had transported him was a gift from his parents that had been sitting on his desk every day. He looked up and tried to get a bearing on where he was. Because of the speed and glow with which he had come through the atmosphere, he hadn't noticed that the color of the sky on the planet was purple. It was beautiful and different from the blue sky he had seen every day of his life. He tried to look away, but he could not. He just kept looking up, mesmerized by the beauty. The purple sky had yellow clouds floating through it, in contrast to the white clouds of Earth; however, the shapes of the clouds looked almost identical to those on his home planet.

Christopher finally took his eyes off the sky long enough to look at the surface he was standing on. He realized the surface was not dirt, grass, concrete, or anything else he had seen in Chicago. The surface had a dark blue color to it, not as dark as a navy but darker than a royal blue. It was another color he had never seen before in his life. He bent down to touch it and was shocked to discover it had a texture similar to snow back on Earth. The only difference, besides the color, was that it was not at all cold. Christopher walked slowly through the soil of the new planet. He noticed that it felt the same as walking through snow. It also made the same distinct crunching sound.

"Amazing!" Christopher said finally. "Everything is so different here. It is so beautiful!"

"That's what these beings would say if they came to your planet."

"Mike?" Christopher said.

Mike appeared, standing right next to Christopher. "It's funny, isn't it? You look at the beauty of your own world so often you start to take it for granted. This world is different from yours, Chris, but no more or less beautiful. Just simply different."

"Very different," Christopher said. "Did you just say 'these beings'? There is life on this planet? I knew it. I knew there had to be life on other planets. Where are they?" Christopher was excited.

"They are just over the hill there, but I warn you: they look much different from you," Mike said.

"Why? Are they green?" Christopher asked.

"No, they're not green, kid! You watch too many movies if you think that every other planet has little green people. The green ones are in a completely different galaxy," Mike said.

Christopher gave Mike a look of disbelief and skepticism. It was hard to tell if Mike was being serious or sarcastic. The two of them were similar in that way.

"Well, I don't care what they look like; I want to see them," Christopher said, as anxious as a little kid about to enter a toy store.

"I know you do, so just go over there, and walk over that hill. But be careful; remember, you are the visitor here."

"Okay!" Christopher yelled as he started running through the snow-like surface toward the hill. He kicked up the blue soil behind him as he ran faster and faster, knowing that once he got to the top of the hill, he would finally know for sure that there was life on other planets. This must be the reason he had been pulled from his room, he thought to himself. He figured the serious questions Mike had spoken of were his questions concerning other life-forms in the universe. Thoughts raced through his mind as he ran closer to the top of the hill. Mike was still standing in the same spot, watching Christopher run up the hill. He shook his head, almost as if he were laughing at him.

Christopher slowed down with each step he took closer to the top, trying to be more cautious. He realized he didn't know if the creatures on the other side were friend or foe. He reached the top and lay down flat on his stomach on the ground. He peeked his head over the hill to survey what lay ahead. He was speechless at what his eyes saw.

It was a huge city—but not at all like Chicago, New York, or any other city he had seen before. There were huge skyscrapers two to three times taller than the tallest buildings in Chicago. He could not even see the tops of the giant superstructures, as they were so tall they disappeared into the yellow clouds. They were not made out of any type of metal. He strained his eyes to try to decipher what they were made of. They looked almost like transparent glass but with bubbly exteriors, as if surrounded by some kind of invisible force field.

As amazing as the otherworldly architecture was, Christopher found himself marveling at the unique and awe-inspiring skyline. The buildings had a backdrop of tall, jagged gray mountains. They were breathtaking against the purple sky. Christopher's eyes were wide with wonder as he tried to absorb and take in everything there was to see.

"What is this place?" he whispered to himself. He looked over his shoulder to make sure there was no one behind him. He was the only one on the hill, and he proceeded to take a few steps closer to get a better view. He was then able to see the life-forms of the planet going in and out of the huge buildings. They looked just like humans from a distance, going in and out of office buildings to work or huge malls to shop. However, as he got closer and looked more, Christopher could tell the creatures were not human.

Christopher rubbed his eyes to make sure he was seeing clearly. The life-forms were different from anything he had seen on Earth and different from anything he had seen in movies, comic books, or even tabloids at the supermarket. They were humanlike in some ways yet different in others. The first thing Christopher noticed was their skin, including its color and texture. Their skin looked much smoother than human skin, almost like the texture of a seal or a dolphin. Some had skin in different shades of blue; others had skin in different shades of gray. They were not tall by any stretch of the imagination. The tallest one Christopher saw did not seem to be more than five foot five, so they were much shorter than the average height of humans. They had two legs and two arms, just as humans did, but they seemed to have much larger hands and arms. They wore long, shiny, flowing robes. Christopher could tell the males from the females, even though they all wore similar robes. The females had more curves than the males did, just as they did on earth. The women also had hair on the tops of their heads, whereas the men did not. *They look so weird*, Christopher thought to himself.

"And do you think they would think that you look normal?" Mike asked as he appeared next to Christopher.

"Mike! Where have you been? And how did you know I was thinking that?" Christopher asked.

"Keep your voice down, kid. You know, they can see and hear you."

"How did you know I was thinking that?" Christopher again asked, this time whispering.

"Because I can hear your thoughts, Chris. How do you think I knew that you love football, the Bears, and all that? I know you better than you know yourself."

Christopher looked confused and bewildered, but after what he had already been through that night, he was starting to think that anything could be true.

"So what am I thinking right now?" Christopher asked to make sure Mike was being honest.

"You're thinking that you like the jersey I'm wearing and that you want to make sure I'm not playing you or deceiving you," Mike answered, smiling.

"That's so cool!" Christopher yelled.

"I told you, Chris: keep your voice down. Just think your thoughts so the people over there won't hear you," Mike said.

"Well, why can't they see or hear you then?"

"I'm here only for you, Christopher; I am your guide, not theirs. They have no need to see or hear me, but you do. Enough about me—this is your journey, and you must continue on it. Oh, and you weren't brought here to make sure that there is life on other planets. Your journey is far more important than just discovering that. Now, do you see that low mountain over there past all the skyscrapers, near the edge of the city? The one that has the rounded top?"

"Yes, I see it. Why?" Christopher responded.

"I want you to meet me over there. Follow the path on the top of this hill as it winds around all of the buildings. Try not to be seen or heard or make contact with anyone. If one of them does spot you, just be nice. Continue on your path, and above all else, do not be confrontational."

"Why can't you just transport me there like you've been doing all night? That way, there's no chance of me bumping into any of those things!" Christopher said.

"They are not things, Christopher," Mike said in a stern voice. "You can learn a lot from them, which is why you are going to walk to that spot. Your job while you are walking is to observe as much as possible. Make sure you do, because I'll be watching you. Oh, and one more thing: make sure you stay on this path. It's the safe way to get to the meeting point. Do not stray from the path."

"What can I possibly learn from them without interacting with them?" Christopher asked.

"That's what you have to tell me when you get there." With that, Mike again vanished into thin air.

Christopher spun around, looking for him, but it was no use. Mike was gone, and Christopher was alone. He stood there and wondered how far away the meeting point was. At least a few miles, he figured. A collage of thoughts ran through his head. What if he couldn't make it? What kind of dangers were out there waiting for him? What if he got thirsty? What if one of the beings saw him and confronted him?

"Will you stop worrying and start walking? You could have been halfway there by now." Mike's voice echoed above Christopher in a joking and sarcastic tone.

Christopher laughed quietly; he had forgotten that Mike could hear his thoughts. *Sorry, Mike*, he thought to himself. For a minute, he thought about how invasive and intrusive it was for someone to hear his innermost thoughts, but then he remembered how calm and at ease he was in Mike's presence. It was as if he had known Mike all his life, so for some reason, the intrusion didn't bother him anymore.

It seemed natural, and the more he thought about it, the more normal it became. Suddenly, he realized that Mike was probably listening to all those thoughts, and he decided he had better start walking before Mike said something else to tease him. He laughed as he took the first few steps on his walk.

CHAPTER 4

Walking the Safe Path

CHRISTOPHER STARTED HIS LONG WALK after just standing there for a few more minutes to try to comprehend the wondrous sights he was privileged to be witnessing. He tried to be cautious, as the unfamiliar ground crunched with each step he took. Still, he was also trying to observe the beings, as Mike had instructed him to do. Christopher thought to himself that Mike would know if he was lying, so he had to make sure to pay attention to them. Besides, how could his curiosity not have been at an all-time high? Even if Mike had not instructed him to monitor the aliens, he couldn't have helped but view them as much as possible. He was in a strange land that presumably no human had been to before and was seeing things he could not have imagined. He was going to take in as much as his sixteen-year-old mind would let him.

As Christopher came across the first curve along the path, he looked over to see the alien creatures from his closest view so far. He noticed they all seemed to have a subtle glow surrounding them, like an aura of some kind, hovering around their bodies. They all had smiles on their small, triangular faces as they walked past one another. They all seemed to be waving their long arms at each other, as if they were waving hello to everyone they saw. There didn't seem to be any who were angry or upset or trying to ignore the others. They all seemed genuinely happy, Christopher thought to himself.

He kept observing them as he walked along the path. He was so focused that he didn't even see the birdlike creature land and stand right in front of him. Christopher turned his head back to the path and was startled to see four eyes staring back at him from the ground. He realized the eyes belonged to some sort of winged animal, but it was not like any bird he had ever seen. The alien bird turned its head to look at Christopher, as if studying Christopher as much as Christopher was studying it. The bird then smiled at him and flew away. Christopher said to himself, "Even the animals here seem happy. This place is amazing."

Mike's voice then whispered in Christopher's mind: "When was the last time you actually looked at animals back home to see if they were happy or not? The time you just spent looking at that creature was longer than you've looked at an earthly animal in the last ten years."

Christopher didn't say or think anything to dispute what Mike had just said, as he knew he was right and only speaking the truth. Too often, people didn't take the time to look at all the beauty surrounding them on a daily basis. Sometimes there was nothing as therapeutic as looking at and admiring the beauties of nature. The simplest things could sometimes be the most calming, such as hearing the sound of a gentle breeze blowing and rustling the leaves of a tree, watching a light snow fall on a winter day, watching the ocean waves wash up on the shoreline, hearing the sound of a rushing waterfall or a summer rain, or watching an eagle soar through the sky. Nature had given humans things to watch or listen to that could help relieve the stress caused by their everyday lives. The question was, did they take the time to truly notice and appreciate them?

Christopher continued on his walk, winding around the biggest bubble-like building on his path and coming up to what seemed to be the front of the structure. He still had not seen a single being with any expression other than a smile on its face. Strangely, Christopher could feel their tranquility radiating out of their bodies. *Is that the reason for the candescent glow wrapped around them?* Christopher thought to himself. Most of the male and female creatures were walking hand in hand, staring into each other's eyes. It was like something out of a movie, as if all of them had just been struck by Cupid's arrow. Christopher was almost to the front of the building. He felt that the tallest and widest of the buildings must have been important. Not only did the building seem to be the largest, but also, there were many people coming in and out of it nonstop. It had more than triple the amount of traffic of the other buildings.

Christopher came around to the front of the building and could not believe his eyes. He stopped in midstride at the breathtaking sight, which gave him chills throughout his body. Hanging on the outside of the building was an enormous, beautiful cross. It was just like the one he was carrying in his hand. It must have been at least fifty stories tall. The majestic symbol seemed to be made out of some kind of shiny metallic substance. Christopher rubbed his eyes to make sure he was seeing correctly, and when he refocused, the cross seemed to be even more detailed and beautiful. Christopher looked down at the cross in his hand with amazement. Why would another planet have had a building with a cross hanging on it?

Christopher quickly switched into reasoning mode to try to come up with a logical explanation for what he was seeing. He told himself the cross must have had a different meaning on that planet. Maybe the building was a hospital. However, that didn't make sense to him either. He had never seen that many happy people go in and out of a hospital on Earth. He lay down on the ground to take his time and observe more closely to see if he could figure out what the building with the cross on it was. *Why does everyone look so happy while walking in and out of it?* he wondered. After watching for a few more minutes, he realized he was too far away to satisfy his curiosity and discover the significance of a cross on that planet. Christopher knew he had to figure out a way to get closer, but that meant leaving the path he was supposed to follow and risking being seen by the inhabitants of the planet. "I have to go down there," he said out loud.

Christopher sat there wondering how he could run down toward the building without being seen. Since all of the beings were wearing robes, his baggy jeans and T-shirt would definitely stand out in the crowd, not to mention the different skin color and hair he possessed. *Mike told me to make sure I stay on this path to get to the meeting point, but he also said I was supposed to observe and learn from these creatures,* Christopher thought to himself. He decided it wouldn't hurt to take a minor detour from the path. After all, Mike hadn't given him a time limit to make it to the mountaintop. So what if it took a little bit longer? The risk was worth the reward.

Christopher took a few steps off the path and moved closer to the alien city below him. If he could run fast enough, he might be able to duck behind some of the smaller buildings, he thought. That way, he could move closer to the tower with the cross hanging from it. The first small building was about two hundred yards down the hill from where he was. He ran down as quickly and quietly as he could, trying to avoid being seen. He made it to the back of the building. He looked around discreetly to see if anyone had noticed him, and to his surprise, no one had seen him.

He was much closer to both the building and the alien beings now. The glow around the beings was even more visible and distinct now. The glow seemed to affect Christopher in a strange way. It made him feel calm and relaxed. He had just run as fast as he could in a land he didn't know, but his heart was no longer beating at a fast pace. A great peace came over him. The peace became greater the closer he came to the happy people on the strange planet.

He started to daydream about happy memories he had, such as the first time he and his family had gone to Disney World or when his parents had brought his little brother, Joey, home from the hospital after Joey was born. He reminisced about the smell of his grandmother's kitchen when she made him something to eat. He thought about the first home run he had hit in Little League and the look on his father's face after he had hit it. He remembered the whole extended family getting together on Christmas Eve at his aunt's house when he was a small child; he and his cousins had been allowed to open presents from their aunts and uncles as an appetizer to the presents Santa would bring on Christmas morning. His mind seemed to be flashing all of those happy thoughts at the same time.

He thought about one of the best Christmas presents he had ever received: a fully authentic Chicago Bears football uniform for kids. He had been eight years old when he received that gift. The outfit had come with football pants, shoulder pads, a helmet, and a number-thirty-four Walter Payton jersey. He remembered how excited he had been to open it. He had put it on immediately and gone outside with his father that afternoon in the snow to play catch in full uniform. That was not only one of his favorite presents he had ever received but also one of the fondest memories he had.

He thought about how Mike had appeared to him wearing a Walter Payton jersey. Did Mike know that was one of his most cherished memories? Was that why he had worn that jersey? Christopher shook his head as if trying to shake all the happy thoughts and memories out of his mind. "Concentrate, Chris," he said to himself. *This is no time for a trip down memory lane. I have to do what I came here to do so I can get to the meeting point with Mike and get back home*, he thought.

The building with the cross was still two buildings away. It would be easier to get past the next two buildings than it had been to get down the hill in the open. He dashed in the shade from one building to the next, again without being seen. He wondered why none of the creatures had seen him. He assumed it was because he was doing such a good job of staying in the shadows, being stealthy, and moving quickly. However, when he was only ten feet from the enormous bubble building with the cross hanging from it, he realized the real reason he hadn't been seen: no eyes were looking anywhere but at the cross. The thousands of beings walking into the building had two things in common: they were all smiling, and they were all concentrating on and staring at the gigantic, breathtaking cross.

Christopher didn't know what to do next. He was now outside the building he had come to see, but what was his next move? To truly understand what the building was, he would have to get inside. *But how am I going to do that?* he wondered. He had not thought ahead about what his next move would be.

"I need one of those robes," he said.

Just then, Mike appeared in front of Christopher. "What are you doing down here, kid? Didn't I tell you not to leave the path? You are supposed to observe these people, not interact with them."

"Mike! I'm so sorry, but I saw this building and—"

"Kid, remember, I can hear your thoughts; you don't have to speak out loud and draw attention to yourself. I know why you did it. I just wanted to see your face when I asked you what you were doing. I wanted to see how scared you would get, and trust me, it was worth it," Mike said with a huge smirk on his face while trying to hold back laughter.

Very funny, Mike, Christopher thought.

Mike continued. "So you just had to satisfy your curiosity and come see what this building was all about. And now that you're down here, you don't know what to do. You need a robe, huh? Well, why don't you just ask for one?"

What do you mean ask for one? Ask who? Christopher responded.

"Put both hands on the crystal cross you have there in your hand.

Concentrate really hard for a robe so you can see what is inside the building, and then ask for it," Mike said.

Are you telling me that all I have to do is wish for something to this crystal, and my wish will be granted?

"Well, there isn't a genie inside, if that's what you're thinking. However, ask, and you shall receive, Christopher. Ask, and you shall receive." With that, Mike disappeared again.

Christopher felt stupid about putting his hands on the crystal cross to make a wish to it. The cross had been sitting on the desk in his bedroom for the last year and a half, and now he was supposed to make a wish to it? On the other hand, what choice did he have? The cross had been just an object on his desk a few hours ago, but it was the same object that had transported him safely across the stars to another planet.

He put both hands around the base of the crystal, closed his eyes, and pictured himself wearing a robe like the ones the beings wore. It would be a robe with a hood, so he could cover his head and hair. He concentrated hard on the wish and asked for a robe, as Mike had instructed. The crystal cross started glowing in his hands, and when Christopher opened his eyes, he was surrounded by little beads of light everywhere. They came out of the cross and covered his body. The beads began to blend together to make one sheet of light, and when the light diminished, Christopher was wearing the robe he needed. The glow from the cross then dimmed until it was just a piece of crystal again.

Christopher extended his arms to inspect the newly tailored piece of clothing he was wearing. It looked just like the aliens' robes, and it had been created just by his sincerely asking the cross for it. "Where were you when I needed to pass my geometry exam?" Christopher joked to himself while looking at the cross.

Christopher pulled the hood up; put his head down, staring at the blue ground to avoid making eye contact with anyone; and walked along the side of the building until he was at the front doors. He stood there looking up at the larger-than-life cross hanging outside the building. The inhabitants of the planet walked right by him as if he were just another one of them getting ready to walk into the building. He put his head down once again and walked inside the massive structure.

He looked up to see what must have been tens of thousands of the aliens sitting in the building, as if they were getting ready to watch a sporting event. Directly in the center of the building was another cross. It was bigger than the one hanging on the outside of the building. It rose from the middle of the floor to the ceiling of the multistory skyscraper. The building was so tall that the rows of seats seemed to go up farther than Christopher's eyes could see.

He made his way to the left, as if he were going to find a seat. He then ducked and hid in a corner. That way, he would not get trapped sitting next to someone and risk being exposed. He looked around at all the beings and noticed they were smiling even more now. They were even happier inside the building than they had been while walking in. Everyone in the entire building stared at the enormous cross, as though they were little children Joey's age staring up at Santa Claus for the first time.

They all chanted something, but the language wasn't English. He struggled to make out any letters or sounds he could recognize, but it was no use. It was unlike anything Christopher had ever heard before. In movies, he had heard every language from Italian to Russian to German. The language he heard now was nothing like any of those languages. He didn't even hear any similar sounds.

After sitting there for ten minutes, Christopher finally heard a word he understood. As soon as he heard it, he thought he must have imagined it. He kept listening and heard the same word again. It was a name. He knew he had heard correctly this time. But how could it have been? The name Christopher heard—the word the aliens were saying—was Jesus.

Christopher could not believe his ears or eyes. He had traveled to the other side of the universe, to a different planet with life on it, yet he was in a building where the inhabitants were worshipping a cross and saying the name Jesus. *How can they know about Jesus and the cross?* Christopher thought to himself.

His mind started racing, searching for rational explanations. Maybe the aliens had been to Earth to study humankind and brought the religion back with them, he thought. Or maybe they had abducted a human who had told them about it. Those were both logical explanations for how the alien race could have known of a human who had lived more than two thousand Earth years ago. However, Christopher knew those possibilities were farfetched. If they had been able to visit Earth, they were obviously more advanced than humans, so why would they have been worshipping one? It didn't make any sense.

Christopher became slightly annoyed and agitated. He was frustrated that he could not understand any more of what the creatures were saying. He had heard them say *Jesus* around ten times, but he had still not been able to make out another word of the language. *Man, I wish I could just understand them as if they were speaking English,* he thought to himself.

After he had that thought, the cross underneath his robe began to glow again. Christopher saw the glow coming from beneath his robe and then heard a sound that reminded him of a strong wind blowing directly into his ear. The sound lasted for about a second or two in his ear and then stopped. When the wind stopped blowing, he was able to understand everything the aliens were saying. It was as if they were speaking English now. The glow from his crystal cross once again dimmed, having done its job. It once again had granted his wish and delivered what he had asked for.

"Now you're getting the hang of it, kid. Ask, and you shall receive," Mike's calm and soothing voice whispered into Christopher's ear.

Now able to understand the language, Christopher paid attention to what they were saying. He was excited that he could determine how they knew the name of Jesus on their planet. It didn't take long for him to realize he was in that planet's version of a church service. He could not seem to find the leader of the service among the enormous crowd. Every church Christopher had ever been to had had one man or woman leading the crowd in prayers or in a sermon. He had been to Catholic churches, which had priests. He had been to Jewish temples for friends' bar mitzvahs, and they had rabbis. He had been to churches where the spiritual leaders were called ministers, preachers, and pastors. In movies, he had seen Native American leaders called holy men.

Christopher kept looking around the massive building but was not able to see any one person leading the group. The enormous crowd of aliens all seemed to be leading the service in unison. They all spoke the same words, as if they were all somehow connected. The experience was different from anything Christopher had ever heard of or seen. He was amazed at the closeness and love he saw among the beings. It was as if the entire group were experiencing the same feelings and thoughts at the same time, almost as if something unseen were guiding all of them. Christopher knew it was an awesome sight to be witnessing.

The way the congregation worshipped was a new experience to Christopher; however, now that he could understand what they were saying, the words were familiar to him. They said, "Thank you, Lord Jesus, for dying on the cross for our sins," and "Our Father, who art in heaven, hallowed be thy name." Christopher was in disbelief. *Not only does this alien society worship the cross and Jesus, but they also have some of the same prayers we have on Earth.*

Christopher had a strange feeling in that place of worship. He was becoming full of love, patience, compassion, and understanding. The longer he sat in the building with the worshipping aliens, the happier and more emotional he became. He looked around and realized the beings' auras were even brighter than they had been outside the building. He then realized the glow seemed to be radiating from the enormous cross and shooting out to each person. It was as if the cross were filling them with the love and energy they needed to have the beautiful glow surround them.

"Christopher, it's time to get to the meeting point. You have more to see, and we have to get going," Mike's voice said into Christopher's ear.

But why? I think I'm starting to feel something wonderful here, Mike. I need to stay a little longer, Christopher responded in his mind.

"No, Chris. You are not at the same level as these beings. You are not ready to worship the same way they do. You need to leave the building now and get to the meeting place," Mike said.

Okay, Mike, Christopher thought reluctantly.

Christopher wanted to stay to keep observing that race of people. He felt such a close connection to them as he sat there that he didn't even want to think about leaving. But Mike was his guide, and Christopher knew that if he wanted to get home again, he had to listen to him.

As Christopher walked out of the building, everyone inside was so focused on the cross that nobody even noticed him walking out. Even when his hood came off, exposing his human hair, no one caught a glimpse of it. He quickly put the hood back on his head and continued walking out. He could not explain it, but the minute he stepped foot outside the building, a feeling of loneliness came over him. It was as if he had just been connected with something bigger than himself, and now he was all alone in the universe. He had never felt that feeling before, and almost instinctively, he turned to go running back into the building.

Suddenly, Mike appeared right in front of him, blocking the way back into the building. "Chris, you must continue on your journey. This is not the place for you. Now, go on to the meeting point."

Christopher nodded in agreement and walked back toward the path he was supposed to follow at the top of the hill. The farther he moved from the building, the more like himself he felt. However, he missed the sense of belonging he'd had while inside the building. *Was I being brainwashed in there? Is that what this whole feeling was about?* Christopher said to himself.

"Yeah, kid, how did you guess? The plan was to bring you halfway across the universe to a different planet just so they could brainwash you. Even though they didn't know you were there, they were brainwashing you," Mike said sarcastically, and he let out a contagious laugh. "Quit thinking so much, Christopher. Just relax and observe."

Christopher laughed to himself as he realized the ridiculousness of what he had said. He continued walking up the hill and got back on the original path Mike had instructed him to follow. He kept walking through the blue soil of the planet, around the curve in the path. The path led away from the beautiful buildings of the alien city. He continued to look back at the buildings, though they were now a distant blur. Still, even from that distance, Christopher could see two things clearly: the large cross on the outside of the building and the glow of thousands of the alien beings shining upward. The glow was bright and reminded him of the way a neon sign lit up the night sky back on Earth.

He continued walking and saw more of the four-eyed birdlike creatures flying above him. They all seemed to be smiling down on him and whistling a beautiful song as they soared overhead. Off in the distance to his right, he saw what seemed to be some type of forest with treelike plants standing tall. The leaves were a blue color that matched the color of the snow-like soil of the planet.

"Cool," Christopher said to himself. "Just like on Earth. We have green grass and green tree leaves; this planet has blue soil and blue tree leaves. That's awesome." He was proud of himself for making that connection between the planets. He looked up at the purple sky as he continued to walk, and while admiring the beauty of it, he thought of the beauty of his own blue sky back on Earth. He thought about getting back home to see that blue sky, with the beautiful white clouds floating through it. He was so wrapped up in thought that he didn't notice someone standing in front of him.

Christopher looked up and saw one of the robed beings in front of him. He was startled, which in turn startled the creature. "Don't hurt me!" the short creature yelled out. The creature stood only around five feet tall. It put both arms over its head in fear.

"Don't worry, little man. I am not gonna hurt you," Christopher said.

The creature gave Christopher a surprised look. "How can you speak my language?"

"What do you mean? When I speak, you hear your own language?" Christopher asked.

"Yes," the creature answered.

"Oh, that is so cool." Christopher realized that his wish to understand their language had also made them able to understand his. "My name is Christopher. I'm not from around here."

"My name is Ragor. I kind of figured you weren't from around here, with how strange you look," the creature said.

Christopher laughed because just as Mike had said, the creature thought he looked strange.

The creature then continued. "I should have known you wouldn't hurt me. Not when you are carrying that around with you." Ragor pointed to the crystal cross.

"Yeah, I figured you would notice this. Hey, why aren't you in that building with those other people?" Christopher asked.

"Actually, I was just on my way there."

"Oh, that place is pretty cool. I snuck inside to take a look, and I have to admit I was very impressed. I do have to ask you something. Why do you think I won't hurt you just because I have this cross?" Christopher said.

"Because if you are carrying that, I assume you must be a believer in the teachings. One of the most important teachings is 'Love thy neighbor as thyself.' Even though we look different, we are still neighbors in a way. That's how I know you won't hurt me."

"I never would have thought that way. When I first saw you, I was startled because I thought you were going to attack. I can tell how peaceful this place is, and I was still on the defense. It's cool that you see things in that way," Christopher said.

"You are on a journey, aren't you? You have been brought here from your planet to observe things, right?" Ragor asked.

"How did you know that?"

"Let's just say I've heard stories. Well, in that case, I really shouldn't be talking to you too much. You have to keep observing, and I don't want to get in the way. Let me just say it was a pleasure meeting you, and may God protect you on your journey." With that, Ragor started walking away from Christopher back toward the city.

"Wait! I have more questions for you, Ragor," Christopher said.

"I'm sure you do, Christopher. And I wish I could answer them for you. Unfortunately, I am not the one to give you the answers. I promise you that if you keep observing, you will find the answers you seek. Remember one thing for me. The teachings say that 'Many are called, but few are chosen.' Christopher, you look like you've been chosen. Be proud and honored for what you are seeing." Ragor turned and continued walking away.

Ragor kept walking the opposite way on the path, and Christopher just stood there watching him. Christopher felt close to Ragor for some reason and was sad he didn't have more time to spend with him.

The aura Ragor exuded must have been rubbing off on Christopher, as he felt the feeling of love and understanding once again. But Christopher knew he had to get to Mike, and Ragor seemed to think he shouldn't answer his questions. How had he known that Christopher was on a journey from another planet, and what had he meant when he'd said he had heard stories? Christopher wanted to ask those things, but since he knew he couldn't, he turned around to continue on his path. Then Christopher suddenly turned around as he heard Ragor yell something at him.

"Oh, one more thing, Christopher! Beware of the Orgilep," Ragor warned. With that, he waved his long arm and turned to keep walking away.

"Beware of the what?" Christopher yelled back.

It was too late; Ragor could no longer hear him. Christopher stood there trying to understand what Ragor had said, but he hadn't gotten the last word. "Oval Rep? No, that wasn't it. Oral strep? No, that wasn't it either. What was it? What did he say?" Christopher asked himself. Then it came to him. "Orgilep. I'm positive he said Orgilep. Now, what in the world is an Orgilep?"

Christopher kept walking for about another mile. He was now closer to the mountaintop where he was supposed to meet Mike. In just a few hundred more yards, he would be there. There was one more big curve to go around, and then he'd see Mike there waiting. The last curve had a big tree along the side of the path. Christopher was just starting to walk underneath the tree, when all of a sudden, something leaped out at him. It was some type of alien beast. It had sharp teeth and claws that looked as if they could have sliced Christopher into little pieces. Christopher fell to the ground, trying to avoid the attack of the creature as it jumped from the tree. Christopher climbed back to his feet immediately. He stared at the creature as it walked toward him. It seemed to be some kind of catlike animal. It was similar to a lion or tiger back on Earth but different, as it had six legs and two tails. It had a muscular build, and its one eye seemed to look right inside Christopher. It was as if the animal knew Christopher didn't belong there, and it was going to make him pay.

It leaped at Christopher. Christopher turned and started running in the opposite direction. The catlike creature easily could have caught him from behind, but it seemed to want to take its time with its prey. Rather than pouncing on Christopher from behind as he ran, the alien jumped over Christopher's head and landed right in front of him again. Christopher skidded to a stop to avoid running into the large creature. He turned to run back the other way as fast as he could. Again, the alien cat jumped over Christopher's head, this time kicking him in the back with one of its six legs. Christopher fell down to the ground from the blow to his back. As he fell, his crystal cross fell to the ground in front of him. Christopher looked at the cross, which was about five feet away from him. An additional five feet from the cross was the alien cat. The cross was directly between the predator and the prey.

The muscular creature ran at Christopher, but as it came to where the cross was, something happened. The crystal cross began to glow, blinding the alien cat with its radiance. Just then, Christopher heard Mike's voice in his head: *"Though you walk through the valley in the shadow of death, you shall fear no evil, for thou art with you."*

The blinding light from the cross seemed to confuse the alien cat. It tried covering its one eye with its paws, but it could not. The light was too intense. The creature had no choice but to run off, leaving Christopher and his cross alone on the path once again. As the creature ran off into the forest below, the glow from the cross once again dimmed, until it returned to its natural crystal state.

Christopher sat there on the ground for a few moments, replaying in his mind the events that had just happened. He had never been so scared in all his life. He'd thought he was going to die on that alien planet—killed by a creature he did not even know the name of.

"Wait a second," Christopher said. "That must have been the Orgilep thing Ragor warned me about. Man, I wish he had been a little more specific about what to expect. That thing was going to kill me."

Finally, Christopher stood up and brushed the snow-like blue soil from his body. He checked his arms and legs to make sure he was not injured anywhere. He was fine aside from some soreness on his back where the Orgilep had kicked him. It would probably leave a bruise but nothing major. The Orgilep's claws had never penetrated Christopher's clothing. Christopher realized the creature had been toying with him, not wanting to make the kill right away. The Orgilep had planned to make it a slow and painful death. Christopher was the mouse the alien cat had decided to play with before making a meal out of him. Christopher walked over to his cross, which was still sitting on the ground. He bent down to pick it up, looked at it in his hand, and said thank you to it, as it had just saved his life. The cross he had tried to hide in his desk drawer a few hours ago had just saved him from an imminent death.

Christopher walked past the tree the Orgilep had jumped out of. He walked past it with caution, afraid there could be another creature waiting to pounce on him. He felt the fear one experienced when anticipating that something bad was about to happen. Luckily, there were no more surprises hiding in the tree.

Christopher went around the last curve and arrived at the rounded mountaintop where Mike had told him to go.

"Mike, I'm here!" Christopher yelled out. "Where are you?"

"Right behind you, Christopher," Mike responded.

Christopher turned around, and there was Mike, sitting on the ground behind him.

"You don't need to wear that anymore," Mike said.

As he said that, Christopher's robe disappeared, and he was once again in his normal clothes. "So you made it," Mike said.

"Barely," Christopher responded. "You told me this path was safe. Did you see that Orgilep thing that tried to kill me?"

"This path is safe, Christopher. No matter how safe a path appears to be, there is always some danger. That is why any path you take in life you never want to take alone. I think you realize you weren't alone on the path now, don't you?"

"No, I wasn't alone. I had my cross with me. It saved my life. It protected me," Christopher said.

"The cross is just an object; the power behind it saved and protected you. That is why you weren't alone," Mike said.

Christopher thought about that for a minute. The power behind the cross had saved him. Christopher let that sentence soak into his mind. *The power behind the cross.* He hadn't really considered that. It was just a piece of crystal back on Earth, so it made sense that something was giving it power. Could that power have really come from Jesus himself?

Christopher then switched subjects back to what Mike had said about the paths people took. He said, "Mike, speaking of paths, why did you allow me to leave the path and go down into the city? You obviously knew I was doing it and why I was doing it. So why didn't you try to stop me?"

"Because sometimes we all must stray from the paths we feel are safe and comfortable to find the truth. You needed to search for something, and that meant straying from what I told you was safe. That takes courage. The important thing is that once you discovered what you were looking for, you went back to follow your path. As you saw, even the path you thought was safe had a hazard on it, but you still made it to your destination without being harmed," Mike said. "So what did you observe from this race of people? What did you discover about them?"

Christopher stood there in thought for a few moments, trying to put what he had witnessed into words. Finally, he looked at Mike, smiled, and said, "They all seemed so happy and full of love. It looked like some of them were strangers to one another, but they still smiled and waved to each other. They had an aura surrounding them that seemed to show the world how full of bliss they were. Inside the building with the cross on it, they all seemed to be connected, as if they were all experiencing the same feelings. They didn't even notice me coming in and out, because they were so focused on what they were doing there. As I was sitting in there, I realized I didn't even need to wish for that robe. I could have walked in there dressed the way I was, and they still wouldn't have noticed or cared. Their attention was on that cross, not on anything else."

"Did you notice anything else?" Mike asked.

"Yes, the longer I was in there, the more I felt connected to them somehow. And when I left, I felt a loneliness that I had never felt before. It didn't make sense to me, and I wanted to go back inside. Why did I feel that way?" Christopher asked, confused.

"Because you *were* connected to them. Like I said, these beings are at a different level of prayer and worship than humans are on Earth. You felt a small piece of that while you were in the building."

"So is it like Sunday here or something? Was that their church service going on?" Christopher asked.

"Yes, it was something similar to what you would call a church service. However, it is not Sunday here. They do this every day on this planet," Mike said.

"Every day? So this wasn't a special occasion or something? Why were there so many people then, and why do they do this every day?" Christopher asked.

"Because on this planet, they have realized that the key to life is to be happy, love one another, and live in peace. By worshipping together like that, they become one—one group worshipping together, just as you picked up on. By being one, they can truly live in peace and harmony together. They have realized that all of their lives are intertwined in one way or another, even if they don't know exactly how. They have also learned to love one another unconditionally, even if they don't know each other or look the same. Take the friend you met along the way here, Ragor. He didn't really judge you because you look different. He just saw another child of God. He saw you, accepted you, and liked you. But as I said, this race is on a higher plane of learning and understanding Jesus's message than humans are on Earth. Of course, they've been doing it a lot longer as well."

"What do you mean they've been doing it a lot longer? And I still don't understand how this planet knows of Jesus. How is that possible?"

"Good questions, Chris. Really, they are. But it is not time to answer those yet. It is time for you to continue on your journey. You are ready for your next lesson," Mike said.

"Next lesson? You mean I'm not going home yet?"

"Not yet, Chris. You still have more to see. I'll meet you there."

Mike once again disappeared.

Christopher stood there alone with only his cross in his hand. He thought about what Mike had just said for a second, and then it hit him. "Meet you where, Mike? You didn't tell me where to meet you!" Christopher shouted.

Just then, the crystal cross started to glow in his hand once again.

"Oh no," Christopher said. "Not again."

Christopher felt everything start to spin around him. He knew what was about to happen next. He clutched on to the cross as tightly as he could, and then it pulled him upward into the planet's purple sky. Just like before, he had no control over where it took him or in which direction the cross went.

"Where am I going now?" Christopher shouted, half scared and half excited.

CHAPTER 5

Another Happy Place?

T HE CROSS PULLED CHRISTOPHER OUT of the planet's atmosphere with the same speed it had pulled him into it, and he was surrounded by the cocoon of light the cross made around him. He was moving through space again, passing other stars, planets, and galaxies. He knew he was moving faster than the speed of light. In what seemed to be only a few minutes, he unknowingly traveled across twenty-seven galaxies, as well as 101 solar systems. Then, just as before, the cross stopped glowing.

Christopher came to a sudden halt and floated there in space, hovering over a different planet the way a helicopter hovered effortlessly above the ground. This planet was different from the last one he had been transported to. This planet had colors of red, black, and yellow in it. It was much smaller than the last planet as well. This planet seemed to be roughly the same size as Earth or maybe even a little smaller. The crystal cross lit up once again and proceeded to pull him down into the new planet. It pulled him through the planet's atmosphere, and once again, he was traveling incredibly fast, with the same white glow surrounding him.

The white glow vanished, the light of the cross extinguished, and Christopher safely landed feet first on another strange new planet.

Once again, Christopher looked around a planet other than his own, trying to get his bearings. The sky was a dark yellow color, much different from the blue of Earth or the purple of the previous planet. He looked off into the distance and saw what seemed to be an ocean of some kind. The water was a strange dark color that looked nearly black. It had waves just as the oceans on Earth did, but they seemed to move much more slowly and powerfully. The waves stood as tall as fifty feet on a regular basis, and even though they moved slowly, when they broke, the power behind them caused a sound similar to the crashing of thunder during a bad storm.

"I don't think even the bravest or most experienced surfer would try to ride one of those waves," Christopher said. He couldn't stop staring at the terrifying alien ocean.

He then looked down at the surface he was standing on. It was a gravel-like substance that was deep red in color. He took a couple steps on the strange new surface, and with each step, a puff of red dust was kicked up. Christopher wondered if it was similar to the surface of Mars.

"No, Mars is more of a rocky surface and does not kick up dust like this does. Plus, Mars doesn't have any oceans on it anymore," Mike said as he appeared to Christopher's left.

"I was wondering when you were going to show up," Christopher said with a smile. "This planet sure is different from the last one. It's still beautiful, but it's a different kind of beautiful, with the ocean and everything. Ya know what I mean?"

"I do know it's different," Mike said.

"So what am I supposed to do here?" Christopher asked.

"Sort of the same thing, kid. Look at the ocean straight ahead. Now look over to your right. Do you see the group of rocks far off in the distance with the waves crashing down in front of them?"

"Yeah, I think I see them. The ones over there?" Christopher pointed into the distance.

"Yes, Chris. That's it. Meet me over there at those rocks. Walk along this shoreline until you get there. Watch out for the waves crashing down. They are much stronger than the waves on Earth, and you could get sucked into this ocean and never come out. Your human muscles would not be able to swim in there," Mike warned. "Remember, you are not to make contact with the life on this planet. Observe them, and when you reach the rocks, I want you to tell me what you have seen from them. Understand?"

"Yeah, Mike, I got it. Don't worry. No one saw me on the last planet, did they?" Christopher said in an arrogant tone of voice.

"You mean except for Ragor, of course," Mike said.

Christopher couldn't believe he had walked right into that line.

Mike continued. "Confidence is a good thing, Christopher. Overconfidence, which leads to arrogance, is not. I'll see you there." Mike was gone again.

"I think I may be starting to get used to him coming and going like that. If I am, it's kind of scary," Christopher joked to himself.

He began walking along the shoreline, as Mike had instructed. He saw that there was some kind of town off in the distance. It was directly between where he was now and where he was supposed to go. There were no skyscraper buildings on this planet, he noticed. He wondered what the aliens on this planet would look like. Would they be anything like the ones on the last planet? Would they be full of love and happiness too? He kept walking, kicking up the red dust with every step. He thought the planet was kind of neat as he looked at the red dust floating in the air over by the black ocean. The red and black against the backdrop of the dark yellow sky was a sight to see.

As he continued to walk, he noticed he hadn't seen any kind of plant life anywhere yet. No trees, no grass, no bushes—nothing. He hadn't even seen a bird flying in the sky. He thought it didn't really matter as long as he didn't see a catlike creature like the Orgilep or anything else that attacked him. He wondered if he would ever be able to look at a lion or other big cat again without feeling the fear he had felt at the moment of the attack. However, just after that thought, he remembered how the cross had protected him at the moment he was most vulnerable. Without Christopher even asking for it, the power of the cross had kept him safe. He hoped that whenever he felt fear the way he had with the Orgilep, he would also feel the comfort of knowing how it had saved him.

Christopher looked down at the cross in his hand and once again said thank you to it. It seemed to shimmer back a light at him, as if it were silently saying, "You're welcome."

Christopher was coming closer to the town he had seen from the distance. It was off to the right of the shoreline he was walking along. He saw small hut-like structures made of some kind of stone. He noticed that none of the structures seemed to be well maintained; it looked as if most of them were falling apart. There was only one building more than three stories, and Christopher could tell it once had been much taller. It looked as if most of the stories of the building had been knocked over somehow.

That building looks like it was purposely demolished. Purposely destroyed, he thought. There were broken stones and rocks surrounding the remaining two stories of the building. On part of the building that had been destroyed, he noticed a design of some kind. Christopher couldn't see what it was from where he was standing. He continued walking along the shoreline, hoping to get a better look as he got closer. He noticed that the dark yellow sky was somehow even darker over the small town. He thought that maybe the destruction of the buildings had made the sky darker, similar to how pollution could cloud the sky over big cities.

He was now only a few blocks from the town. He could see the life-forms of the planet walking around the town. They looked much different from the beings on the last planet.

The creatures on this planet had a more human look than those on the last planet. Their skin seemed to be similar to that of humans, with the exception that their skin was a rusty red color. Their muscles were much bigger and much more defined. Their shoulders were very broad and square, making the overall appearance of their bodies much wider. They had gill-like features on the sides of their necks, probably so they could still breathe while swimming in the forceful and treacherous waters of the black ocean. Christopher noticed the height of the aliens. The shortest one he could see stood about six and a half feet tall. They all had jet-black hair, but the women's hair was much longer. The hair was more like a horse's mane than the hair on a human's head. Christopher noticed that with their dark reddish skin and black hair, they could blend into the planet when needed. It was as if they were born with the perfect camouflage outfits. They wore clothing, but it looked more like some kind of armor. The armor covered their chests and groin areas, leaving their muscular arms and legs free to be both seen and feared.

Christopher continued along the shoreline, hoping to see a little bit more of the creatures. After all, he was supposed to be observing them. The shoreline did not come any closer to the town; it stayed at a distance of around two blocks away. He wanted to move closer. He needed to know how else they were different from humans and also how they differed from the aliens on Ragor's planet. He decided he could walk off the shoreline, hiding between some of the stone huts.

As he took his first steps toward the town, Mike appeared in front of him.

"Christopher, I allowed you to leave the path you were supposed to take on the last planet, but I cannot allow you to on this planet. It is not wise to make a habit of constantly straying from the paths you are supposed to follow. That's how people get confused and led astray," Mike warned.

"Mike, I have to go see these creatures. It worked out fine for me the last time. No one ever knew I was there," Christopher responded.

"Just because something works out for you once doesn't mean it will always turn out the same way. If you want to go satisfy your curiosity, I cannot stop you. This is your journey, and as I've said, I'm only your guide. However, I must warn you: if you go into that town, I will not be able to make contact with you again until you reach the meeting point," Mike said.

"Why not?" Christopher said, slightly annoyed.

"Because I simply cannot follow you if you decide to go down there. That is all I can tell you as to why. I am your guide on this path. If you stray from it, I cannot go with you. I'm sorry," Mike said humbly.

"Will this still work if I leave this path?" Christopher held out his crystal cross.

"Yes, Christopher. The power you carry with you there is always with you."

"Well, I'll be fine then. I'll meet you where you said as soon as I look around here a little bit more. How often does someone get an opportunity like this, Mike? I have to take advantage of it, or I will never forgive myself. I'll be fine, and I'll meet you at the rocks soon." Christopher started to walk toward the town.

"Be careful, Christopher," Mike said in a concerned voice.

Christopher had listened to Michael's warning, but his desire to learn and understand things drove him to go find out everything he could about the beings. He felt safe after witnessing the power of his crystal cross and the way it had protected him from the attack of the Orgilep on the last planet. He felt invincible while carrying the cross now. Power had a way of making people feel that way in all aspects of life—they tended to feel that nothing could hurt them or touch them if they had power. That feeling could lead people to become corrupted by the power they possessed if they were not careful.

Christopher ran from the shoreline's edge to the first stone hut on the edge of the town. As the yellow sky was darker over the town, it provided more shadows for Christopher to move through. He was now within range to view the life-forms on the planet at a close distance.

At first, it seemed the beings were just as full of happiness as the beings on the other planet. They seemed to be smiling constantly. Christopher even saw quite a few of them hugging one another as a gesture of love, he thought.

However, looks could be deceiving, especially from a distance. What Christopher had interpreted as happiness and smiles were actually looks of anguish and hatred and frowns. What he had interpreted as hugs were actually fights breaking out around the entire town.

Christopher was shocked to see the creatures fighting one another. The environment was the exact opposite of the last planet he had visited, on which everyone had been full of love. These were not fights like schoolyard fights that broke out. It was like watching two dogs fight each other in a pit. The fighters displayed pure animal instinct. The fights were the only-the-strong-survive, kill-or-be-killed kind of fights. Their fighting was the most violent thing Christopher had ever seen in his life. It was more violent than he ever could have imagined. *No wonder Mike told me to be careful*, he thought to himself.

Beyond the many fights going on, something caught Christopher's eye. Off to his left, he saw the multistory building that had been partially destroyed. He snuck around the backs of two more hut-like structures until he was only a few feet from the demolished building. He was finally able to see the symbol lying on the ground. It appeared the symbol might have been the reason the building was intentionally demolished. When Christopher finally saw the symbol, it took his breath away: it was a giant stone cross.

Christopher felt a flood of different emotions. *Another planet and another building with a cross on it?* he thought to himself. *How do these other planets know of the cross, and why was this building destroyed because of it? Maybe this time the cross does have a different meaning.* Then he wondered what it would mean if the cross did symbolize the same thing on this planet as it did on Earth and on Ragor's planet. What if it was a symbol of Jesus and the love promised by God, and it had been purposely demolished?

He stood there in the shadows, looking at the destroyed building. He looked at the enormous cross that once had hung on the building, possibly an emblem of hope and promise. It had fallen and now lay on the ground among the rubble. Christopher felt a great sadness come over him suddenly. The pain seemed to actually hurt his heart. His eyes became teary, and he pondered why the cross had been discarded. He wanted to go over to the fallen cross to give it a hug, as if it were a person who had been hurt or injured.

He was in such a state of sadness that he didn't realize he was no longer standing in the shadows but had wandered out into the open, in plain view. He also didn't notice the huge inhabitant of the planet sneaking up behind him.

Christopher all of a sudden got a feeling he was being watched. Growing up in the city, he had learned to trust natural instincts like that, as they more often than not were accurate. He looked around and finally realized he was no longer being stealthy and hiding in the darkness but had allowed himself to become distracted and walk right into the open, where he could be seen. Luckily, the creatures off to his right were so busy fighting that they hadn't noticed him. They were the opposite of the people on the other planet: the others hadn't noticed him because they'd been so focused on the cross; here they didn't notice him because they were too busy fighting and trying to kill each other. Still, Christopher had an uneasy feeling in his gut.

He started taking steps backward to retreat into the safety of the shadows. He made it without being seen back into the shadows between two of the stone huts. It reminded him of being in an alley between two houses at home.

He turned around—and saw one of the big creatures running at him from a distance of only about twenty feet away. The creature was charging him at full speed, with muscles flexed, mouth open, and fists clenched, ready to attack. Christopher didn't have any time to react, but he knew he could not run out into the open, as that would have brought the risk of more of the creatures seeing him and trying to attack him. He unknowingly and instinctively got into a stance to defend himself from the imminent attack.

The creature was now ten feet away, and he was yelling something at Christopher. Of course, Christopher couldn't understand the language, nor did he care what was being yelled at him. His only thought was how he would get out of the situation.

Christopher knew the creature was much stronger than he was, as it was apparent the creatures would have been much stronger than any human on Earth. It was much broader, wider, and more muscular. Then he wondered whether or not it was faster than he was.

Christopher had learned with his experiences in street fighting that one always had to find the advantage against an opponent. If the opponent was stronger, Christopher was usually faster. If the opponent was faster, Christopher was usually stronger. If the opponent was stronger and faster, Christopher was usually smarter. If the opponent was stronger, faster, and smarter, he needed to rely on experience, and a lot of luck, to win the fight.

Those thoughts raced through his mind during the microseconds as the creature approached. The creature was now only five feet from him. The attacker reached out to grab Christopher around the throat.

Christopher ducked underneath the enormous arms of the alien creature, and it ran right past him. The creature was slower than Christopher, and it was much less agile than the smaller human.

The creature skidded to a stop, kicking up red dust underneath its massive feet. It turned back around to begin a new attack against Christopher. Again, it yelled something while running toward him.

Christopher thought to himself, *I wish I could understand this language so I could know what this thing keeps yelling at me.*

After he had that thought, the crystal cross in his hand began to glow again. Christopher saw the crystal illuminate, not even realizing that he had made a wish and that the wish was being granted. He then heard the sound in his ear again, just as before, like a strong, crisp wind blowing. The sound lasted for a second or two, as it had before, and then he was able to understand what the creature was yelling.

The creature was once again closing in on Christopher; it was only ten feet from him now. The creature yelled, "You do not belong here!"

Christopher could not have agreed more, and he knew Mike had been right. He should have stayed along the shoreline, as Mike had warned him to.

"You must die!" the alien shouted as it attacked.

Christopher turned to run and got about ten yards away from the creature before quickly realizing there was nowhere for him to run to. He was cornered in a dead end of the alley-like path, with the only opening leading back out into the open, where there were more of the creatures fighting in a frenzy.

Christopher turned back around and saw the alien still coming toward him, seemingly even more confident, knowing Christopher had no escape route. Christopher did not want to do battle with the creature, but his fight-or-flight response kicked in. His first instinct was to run, but since that was not an option, he instinctively knew what had to happen. There was nowhere for him to go, as running out into the open would have led him to more of the violent creatures, which possibly would have all united against Christopher and attacked him. A rush of adrenaline shot through his body; it was time to stand his ground. It was time for a fight, whether Christopher wanted it or not.

The alien creature again reached out to grab Christopher around the throat. Christopher again ducked underneath the slower creature's attempt to grab him. As he ducked below the creature's arms, he delivered an uppercut punch with his right hand to the creature's stomach area. The creature let out a small groan of pain as Christopher's fist connected with the alien's muscular abs.

Although Christopher was a powerful puncher for his age and size, the creature was able to shake off the punch the way Christopher would have dismissed a punch from his younger brother. The creature, now even angrier after being hit, once more turned and ran at Christopher with its arms extended to grab him. Again, Christopher attempted to duck underneath the creature's outstretched arms. However, this time, the creature expected the move and countered it by grabbing Christopher by the back of his T-shirt. The creature then threw Christopher viciously against the side of one of the stone huts.

Christopher's body slammed against the stone, and he fell down to the ground, dropping his cross from the grasp of his left hand. He tried to stand up, but he was wobbly from the impact of being thrown against the wall with such fury. He had never felt anything like the power and force he had just been thrown with. The creature stood there howling at Christopher, as if it could already taste the victory over the smaller, weaker, and more fragile being. It walked toward Christopher, ready to dish out some more punishment and perhaps even provide a final death blow. The creature's overconfidence and slow walking allowed Christopher to reach out and pick up his cross.

Christopher stood up with the cross in his hand and wished the cross would protect him from the creature and throw the creature with even more force than it had thrown Christopher. The cross began to glow, and Christopher reached out toward the creature and said, "How do you like it now?"

The creature lunged at Christopher, and the cross glowed more intensely. A stream of light shot out from the center of the crystal cross and hit the aggressive creature directly in the chest. The impact from the light threw the creature across the entire length of the alley and slammed it into the wall of the other building. The creature fell to the ground, unconscious from the blow and the impact of the wall.

Christopher was once again in awe. He couldn't believe the ease with which the cross had thrown the enormous creature and knocked it unconscious. He thanked the cross once more for saving his life.

Christopher now had a chance to study the alien up close. He noticed that it had four eyes: two in the front, where humans had them, and one on each side of the head, right above where the ears were located. *The extra eyes must be used in the violent ocean*, he thought, *along with the gills on their necks, so they can see and breathe underneath the humongous and ferocious waves crashing on top of them.* That particular creature was around seven feet tall and probably weighed more than four hundred pounds, without an ounce of body fat. Even while unconscious, the creature seemed to look angry and hateful.

All of a sudden, a noise from the other end of the alley caught Christopher's attention. He turned around and saw two more creatures walking down the other end of the alley between the two huts. He heard them talking; they were looking for their ally, the creature that had attacked him. Luckily, they hadn't yet seen their partner lying there on the ground knocked out, nor had they seen Christopher. Christopher knew he had to get out of there before he was spotted. He frantically looked around the alleyway to see if there were any windows or openings he could crawl into, but unfortunately, there was nowhere to hide. His only choice was to run back out into the open toward the demolished building with the fallen cross in front of it. Some of the brawls that had prevented him from leaving before had moved away from the building, giving him a better chance of making it without being seen. He ran out from the safety of the shadows into the open space.

Christopher made it to the destroyed building and ran inside through the two broken front doors. Now safe from the dangers that lurked outside the building, Christopher took time to look around the broken-down structure. He hoped to find out why it had been demolished and what the meaning of the cross was on that planet.

It seemed the structure had been destroyed decades ago or maybe even hundreds of years ago. It was depressing to be in there. Christopher had been around many condemned buildings in Chicago, but they didn't compare to the devastation of this one. There was a feeling of despair and disappointment coming from the building, as if it never had gotten a chance to fulfill its purpose. Christopher walked up broken and cracked concrete stairs to reach the second floor. He looked down on the first floor and imagined the carnage that must have taken place in order to bring down a building of that size. What acts of violence had been performed in that place, and what had been the reason for the demolition? Then Christopher heard a strange voice scream, "What are you doing in here?"

CHAPTER 6

An Unlikely Friend

CHRISTOPHER TURNED AROUND TO SEE another one of the large creatures standing behind him. This creature was a little bigger than the last one, standing at least seven feet three inches in height, and it seemed to be outraged that Christopher was in this building. "What are you doing in here? Get out of here!" the creature yelled.

Christopher didn't know whether to stand and fight or run out of the building. If he stayed and fought, there was only one creature to worry about. If he ran back outside, there were hundreds, and he knew that at least three would be looking for him. Christopher decided to stand his ground. He clenched his crystal cross in his right hand, ready to defend himself. The creature continued to yell at him.

"Get out of here! I don't know what you are, but I'm not going to let you destroy this building any more than it already is!" the creature said.

"Destroy this building? I don't want to destroy this building! I am a visitor here, and I was curious about what happened to it. I'm only in here because I'm hiding from some of your kind who attacked me outside," Christopher said.

"What is that in your hand? Why are you carrying that? Where did you get that?" the creature asked, pointing to Christopher's cross.

"It's a cross. It brought me here from a faraway planet called Earth, where I am from."

"You're from another planet? Well, that explains why you look so weird," the creature said.

Christopher laughed at the thought of the alien creature saying he looked weird. His laughter was contagious, and the creature started to chuckle as well. The creature realized it must have looked as strange to Christopher as Christopher looked to it.

"What is your name, my young traveler from another planet?" the creature asked in almost a friendly tone.

"My name is Christopher. You can call me Chris. What is your name?"

"My name is Sitrof. It's nice to meet you. Please tell me, Chris—what do your people know of the symbol of the cross?"

"Well, some people on my planet believe that the Son of God was put to death on a cross to save the world from sin. The son's name was—"

"Jesus?" Sitrof said anxiously, wanting to know if it could be true.

"Yes, how did you know that? Is that the same meaning of the cross that hung from this building before it collapsed?" Christopher asked.

"Yes, this building was to be a place for my people to come worship our Lord and Savior, the Son of God, Jesus. He came here to save our planet from sin as well."

"You might not believe this, but I just came from another planet that believes in Jesus, just like mine does. This is the third planet I've been to today, and all of them have at least some believers who feel Jesus came to save them."

"Three planets? That is a confirmation, you know," Sitrof said.

"How do you mean?" Christopher asked.

"What are the chances that three different planets galaxies apart would all believe in the same God? And that the same God would send his Son with the same name of Jesus to all of the planets? What would be the chance if it weren't true? God obviously sent his Son to all of these planets because he loves all life that he created. That's how I see it," Sitrof said.

"Well, if that's true, why does this planet have so many problems? I mean, the last planet I visited was full of love and peace—I could believe that. But how can we believe it when we see your people here?" Christopher said.

"Because of the free will that God gave us, I suppose. We are all free to choose whether or not we believe. After the death of Jesus, many people here believed he truly was the Son of God. They believed in his message of love, patience, and understanding. Unfortunately, it didn't take long for the love he taught us to be forgotten. Many of our people were afraid to believe and afraid to let love into their hearts. This lack of faith led to an eventual uproar of hatred that spread throughout what was once a beautiful planet. 'Love thy neighbor' quickly turned into 'Love thyself.' They rejected everything Jesus stood for, and they would never believe in God. To them, there could be no being more powerful and important than themselves. Soon all anyone cared about was what could improve their lives, no matter who they had to hurt or kill to get it. As you can see, our planet is now one constant battle. Even when there is nothing to fight and kill over, they fight and kill anyway. This way, there is one less enemy to worry about in the future, when there might be something to fight about."

"So then why do you seem so calm and logical?" Christopher asked.

"I am one of the few left who still believes in what Jesus came here to teach us. We are constantly hunted by the others who do not believe, as we are just something else they want to kill and destroy. They will try to destroy us just like they destroyed this building. They first ripped down the cross that hung outside and then demolished the building from the inside out. Sometimes they come back just to make sure no one tries to rebuild anything. Even if nothing has been rebuilt, they destroy a little bit more just in case. That is what I thought you were doing here—trying to destroy more of this place."

"Well, what are you doing here then?" Christopher asked.

"Even though it is destroyed, I still like to come here and imagine what it could have been like. It could have been wonderful. Can you imagine if everyone out there fighting put that much energy into praying? What a different world it would be," Sitrof said.

"How long has it been like this? Ya know, with the fighting and killing."

"For thousands of years. Slowly, the believers died out or were hunted and murdered. Now there are less than forty of us left on the entire planet. We still try to spread the Word when we can, but it is hard to convince people motivated by greed, anger, and hatred to believe in something they can't see. To convince them to believe in something that doesn't give them instant gratification. To believe in something they have to have blind faith in is almost impossible here. We had our chance, and we blew it. While I don't want to give up hope, I fear that soon the believers, me included, will all be wiped out. And then chaos will rule this land unchallenged forever and ever."

"What made the majority of the people turn to this life of hate and death? I mean, why would anyone choose to live a life of constant war?"

"Simple. They found that it made more sense not to believe. It was easier to believe there isn't something greater than they are. It was more logical, they thought at the time. All that talk of love was silly to them. And as you may know, the absence of love is the breeding ground for hate. It is so much easier to believe the negative things you hear than the positive. This negativity led to anger, which in turn boiled into pure hatred, and then the hate inevitably was followed by numerous wars. First, there were wars over which version of religion was better. Then came wars over which religion was wrong. Next were wars over why we shouldn't bother to teach any religions. The ironic part is, they wanted to stop teaching religions so there wouldn't be reasons to fight over them. The thinking at the time, as I understand it, was that if religions were not taught, everyone could decide for themselves what they wanted to believe in.

However, before long, all talk of religion resulted in being severely punished. Eventually, any discussions, displays, or expressions of religion were punishable by death. After a while, the name of Jesus was all but lost; people were unable to speak it, for fear of being killed. The people who still believed after that were labeled as weak and soft. The slaughters began, and they were brutally executed. Next thing you knew, there were no longer any consequences to people's evil actions. They had succeeded in actually making it easier for people to kill one another. They killed over land, mates, food, looks—it didn't matter. Hatred had taken over their hearts, and their souls were gone. It has been going on for so long now that this is what they think life is supposed to be like. 'Survival of the fittest,' 'Only the strong survive,' and all that nonsense. They look at love and the name of Jesus as a threat to that way of life. If only they knew that he is the life." Sitrof had a sad look in his eyes.

Christopher held his head down low. He felt horrible for the pain Sitrof felt. Christopher had the right to believe in Jesus back home and really didn't, while Sitrof was willing to die because he believed in him so much.

"I'm so sorry for what has happened to your planet. Is there any chance it could change one day?" Christopher said.

"There is always a chance, Chris. That's what faith teaches us," Sitrof said with a smile. "I sure hope it does. I think of Jesus and the Father sitting there in heaven, looking down on us, and I know they must feel saddened by what we have become. If things don't change in my lifetime, at least I know I'll live forever in heaven, in paradise. I'd rather live in misery here for a few decades and then in heaven for eternity than live like the rest of my people do for a few decades and in misery for eternity. It's an easy and clear choice for me. I'm one of the lucky ones here since I know the truth."

Just then, they heard noises coming from right outside the building. They looked out one of the many holes in the concrete walls and saw two of the three creatures Christopher was hiding from: the one he had knocked unconscious with the cross and another one with him.

"There were three of them. They must be looking for me," Christopher said. "I thought you said the attitude is 'Everyone for himself' here. Why are three of them working together?"

"Because they do it out of necessity. Many people make short-term alliances in order to accomplish certain like-minded goals. There are many dictatorships here—groups of warriors led by a single head warrior at the time. The minute something with the group goes wrong, they kill the dictator and delegate a new one, usually by way of a fight to the death. Even people who are full of hatred need some kind of social circle. This has become the way here," Sitrof said. "Chris, don't take this the wrong way, but how did a being as small as you escape from those three killing machines?"

"Well, actually, only one attacked me. The one standing down there on the right was the one I saw."

"Well, that is Tadlos. He is a vicious, thoughtless soldier who lives for the kill. The one standing on the left is Mandar. He is one of the head dictators I told you about. He rules a group of about three thousand. He is absolutely ruthless and is actually one of the longest-reigning dictators in this part of the world. He was even smart enough to create a system of captains so he can rule over many lands without physically being there. It is rare to be able to maintain that large of a group in this world, when there is always someone else wanting to be in charge. But he is an intelligent warrior who is very dangerous. He has never been defeated in battle. In fact, he has never come close to being defeated. Rumor has it is that in more than one thousand battles, he has never even been knocked off his feet. He carries that mighty sword with him to strike fear into would-be opponents."

Christopher looked at the sword Sitrof was talking about. The sword must have been at least five feet long, with a shiny and razor-sharp blade. It had a curved hilt that made it easy for Mandar to swing it around at his victims. It was an amazing weapon and a fearsome sight in the mighty warrior's hands.

"How do you know so much about this Mandar?" Christopher asked.

"Because he has tried to kill me or have me killed many times. He wanted me to join him, but I refused. As you can imagine, being told no is not something a leader like Mandar is used to. From that moment, he swore I would pay for defying him. I have always been blessed and been able to escape. But I have seen him kill entire villages of warriors all by himself. He has declared me his sworn enemy because I have escaped the kill of his sword so many times."

"Well, luckily, this Mandar wasn't there yet when the other one attacked me. Neither was the other one, the one I don't see right now. They came later, after I had escaped. The one you called Tadlos is the only one I encountered."

"How did you escape against such a strong soldier like him?" Sitrof asked. "Tadlos is Mandar's number-one soldier in this section of his reign."

"I really didn't do anything; my cross protected me."

"What do you mean it protected you?"

"I was trying to fight him off and did okay for a minute, but then he got ahold of my shirt and threw me against the wall. I held out my cross, and it shot out a ray of light that knocked the creature out," Christopher said.

"Amazing. And this is the same cross that brought you here and to the other planet you spoke of?

"Yes, the same one."

"Praise God. That cross has been anointed with the power of Jesus, hasn't it?" Sitrof said.

"If you would have asked me that yesterday, I would have thought you were crazy. But after the night I've had, I have to agree that could be true."

"Praise his name," Sitrof said.

All of a sudden, Sitrof was hit from behind with what appeared to be some type of club. He was hit in the back of the head, and the blow knocked him to the ground. It was the third warrior they hadn't seen with Mandar and Tadlos. The creature yelled, "That talk of Jesus is why I have to kill you, Sitrof! Mandar will be quite pleased to know that I not only found this weak alien creature but also killed the elusive Sitrof."

Sitrof tried to get up, but the hate-filled killer knocked him back down. Christopher, without hesitation, ran over to try to help his new friend, who was lying there defenselessly. He jumped and punched the much larger warrior in the back of its head three times. The creature stumbled forward a few feet before regaining its balance. Christopher did not have the strength to do any damage to the aliens of the planet with his punches. The angry creature turned to charge at Christopher.

Sitrof was still unable to get to his feet after the vicious blows he had taken to the head. He picked up a stone and threw it at the creature's back while it ran toward Christopher. The creature turned back to see Sitrof lying there on the ground. It ran up to him and kicked him in what appeared to be the ribs. Christopher again ran over to help Sitrof, but the creature saw him coming, grabbed Christopher by the shirt, and threw him down to the ground like a doll. Christopher slid on his back about ten feet along the concrete-like floor before coming to a stop against the near wall.

The warrior was not at all impressed with Christopher and could not understand how Tadlos had lost to that puny being. The creature then picked up a slab of stone from the ground, held it up over its head, and turned to Sitrof, who was still lying on the ground. "Where is your Jesus to save you now, Sitrof?"

As the creature was about to hit Sitrof with the stone, Christopher held out his left hand, which was holding the cross. The glow from the cross immediately lit up the room, and just as before, a ray of light shot out from the center. The ray hit the massive creature directly in the stomach area and proceeded to carry both the creature and the slab of concrete he was holding approximately twenty feet until they both slammed into the far wall of the building. Sitrof looked in awe as he witnessed firsthand what the cross could do. Just as Tadlos had been earlier, the evil creature was unconscious after being hit with the power of the cross.

Christopher ran over to help Sitrof to his feet. "Are you okay?"

"I think so. Thank you. You saved my life. Thank you, Lord Jesus! That cross you have is indeed powerful," Sitrof said as Christopher helped him up.

"That was the third one I saw with the other two earlier," Christopher said.

"Yes, I know. His name is Allanac; he is another one of Mandar's top soldiers."

"He knew of you?" Christopher asked.

"Of course. Mandar and his group have been trying to kill me for years, remember? I am one of the last believers in this part of the planet. Whoever kills me will be considered a hero by most around here and will almost certainly guarantee himself a longer stay at the side of Mandar," Sitrof said as he looked out the window. "Oh great, it looks like we're not safe yet!"

They looked out to see Mandar and the other creature, Tadlos, turn and walk into the building. "They must have heard the commotion in here. You have to get out of here," Sitrof told Christopher.

"I don't think so, man. You're the one who needs to get out of here. Look, I have the cross; you saw its power. I will be okay. This planet needs you. Like you said, they will definitely kill you if they find you. You have to continue to try to spread love and peace in this world if it is to have a chance. Now, is there a back door out of here you can take?"

"Chris, I can't leave you. What would that say about my character if I left a smaller creature like you here to fight two of my people?"

"It would say that you are smart. It would say that you know the good that is needed on this planet and that you can do here. And it would say that you have trust and faith in the power you have seen in this cross. Now, get out of here. Please let me do this for you. Let me show you there are still people who believe in 'Love thy neighbor.' Even if they are neighbors from other planets," Christopher said with compassion.

"It was an honor to meet you, Chris. I will pray for your safe return to your planet. I hope yours does a much better job of spreading the Word than mine has done. God be with you and bless you."

"You too, Sitrof. Good luck to you."

With that, Sitrof turned and ran out the other side of the building. Mandar and Tadlos were now inside the building. Christopher looked down on them from the second floor. He realized it was the perfect time for a surprise attack. He had a whole floor separating himself from the creatures; if he used the cross against them now, they would never even see the attack coming.

Christopher tiptoed to a place where he would have a clear line of fire to take down the two killers. He held out the cross with his right hand, just as he had done when he was being attacked. He waited for the cross to illuminate with a magnificent glow and for the rays of light to shoot out. He waited patiently, anxious to see the looks on the seemingly fearless creatures' faces as they were struck with the unmatchable power from the cross.

Nothing happened.

Christopher looked at his cross, confused. Why didn't a ray shoot out at the creatures, as it had before? He switched the cross to his left hand and again held it out for an attack. Again, he waited, but no glow came over the crystal.

What's going on? It's not like this thing runs on batteries! he thought to himself, slightly agitated. He was in perfect position for the attack, yet the cross would not follow his commands.

"Come on. I'm wishing for you to attack," Christopher said to the cross.

Still, nothing happened. The cross looked like a regular piece of crystal in his hand. No glow or power came from it. The two creatures were starting to make their way up the stairs. Christopher had lost his chance for the surprise attack. He put the crystal cross in the front pocket of his baggy jeans and looked around for a way to escape.

He saw a hole in the wall to his left. It was just wide enough for him to crawl through. He ran over to it and looked through the hole. It led outside the building, but he was on the second floor. He would have to jump down. He looked down and saw that he could make the jump to the roof of a neighboring hut and then jump down from there without being seen.

Christopher started crawling through the hole just as Mandar and Tadlos made their way to the second floor. He made it through the hole and found himself standing on a ledge outside the building, two stories above the ground.

Mandar and Tadlos saw Allanac lying on the ground unconscious.

"Who is this puny creature that left you unconscious and now has struck down Allanac?" Mandar asked Tadlos.

Christopher knelt down on the ledge to hear the conversation. Mandar had a deep, threatening voice that could have struck fear into anyone. He stood around eight feet tall and was a menacing sight. His muscles bulged larger than those of the other creatures Christopher had seen. He carried his large sword in his right hand, and there was evidence it had recently been used.

"How could this tiny creature have whipped both of you?" Mandar asked.

"He had some kind of weapon that he shot me with. I really didn't see what it was, but it looked like some kind of cross that the weak ones worship," Tadlos said.

"A cross?" Mandar shouted as he slapped Tadlos across the face. "You let one of the weak believers beat you in a fight? I should kill you myself!"

Tadlos hung his head in shame, knowing Mandar might kill him for the embarrassment of losing a fight to someone carrying a cross.

"I'm sorry, Master. It won't happen again," Tadlos said.

"If it does, you'd better hope the believer kills you, because the death he gives you will be much more merciful than the one I'll give you. Now, get Allanac to his feet, and let us find this thing," Mandar said.

Christopher had heard enough. He knew he had to get out of there. Besides, hanging outside a building was a sure way to be spotted by some of the other creatures around. Christopher jumped off the ledge and landed on the roof of a hut down below. He then jumped off the roof and landed safely on the red soil, kicking up a cloud of red dust. He then ran as fast as he could back to the shoreline to get to the meeting point with Mike. He had seen enough of this planet.

CHAPTER 7

The Choices We Make

CHRISTOPHER WANTED TO GO HOME. He had grown up around violence in the city, but he had seen nothing like the untamed carnage and chaos of this planet. In the short time he had been in that town, he had witnessed the brutal killings of dozens of the beings in cold blood. It was disheartening to see that much life lost over nothing. He was also concerned about why his cross had stopped working. How would he be able to make it home if it didn't work? What if another one of the violent creatures attacked him?

Christopher finally made it back to the shoreline next to the black ocean. He looked at the ocean for a minute as the huge waves continued to crash down, making the thunderous sound. *Even the ocean is violent here*, he thought.

He started walking toward the meeting point. He was close and couldn't wait to see Mike. His mind wandered to Sitrof. He hoped he'd made it to safety. He was glad to have met at least one decent being on that planet. In fact, Sitrof was much more than decent. He had been willing to stand and fight so that Christopher, a complete stranger, could escape. Christopher knew he had done the right thing by making Sitrof leave. He felt good about himself. In a way, he felt as if he had actually saved Sitrof. *This planet needs someone like him*, he thought. Maybe Sitrof would be able to make a difference for the better one day.

Christopher rounded the last curve of the shoreline and walked to the rocks where he was supposed to meet Mike. He was careful as he walked slowly along the jagged rocks. He knew that if he slipped, he could fall into the angry ocean. Trying to fight through those ferocious, unforgiving waves was not something he wanted to think about.

Christopher made it to the top rock, and he finally had some solid footing to stand on. Mike appeared in front of him.

"Did you miss me, Chris?" Mike asked.

"I'm just ready to go home. You were right, Mike; I shouldn't have left the path to go into that town. I can't believe the horrible things that happen on this planet," Christopher said.

"I know. It's very sad to look at what could have been a great species now just destroying themselves. I heard your thoughts, and they said you were happy you got to meet Sitrof. If you hadn't left the path, you never would have met him. You must always look at the positive of an experience, not just the negative. The negatives are easier to see, but the positives, while sometimes elusive, can make all the difference."

"I suppose that's true, but the part where I witnessed numerous killings and almost got beaten to death myself are the things that stand out most," Christopher said.

"But you are alive and safe. You showed signs of true bravery in trying to fight those creatures that towered over you."

"Thank you, but I didn't really know what else to do. I put myself in a bad situation, but luckily, the cross got me out of it. Speaking of that, I think I have a problem. The power in this cross is gone. After I stayed to fight Mandar and his soldier so Sitrof could escape, the cross wouldn't work. I tried to attack them with it, and nothing would happen. I had to sneak out of the building without being seen. Why did it stop working?"

"It didn't stop working, Chris; it just wouldn't work for what you were asking it to do."

"Why not? What happened to 'Ask, and you shall receive'?"

"The energy behind that cross is extremely powerful, but it is also extremely good. It cannot be used for an evil purpose."

"So how does that apply to me? How was I trying to use it in an evil way?"

"The power behind this cross is a power of love, understanding, guidance, and protection. It is not a weapon that can be used to attack. Like you said, you had a way to sneak out of the building. There was no reason for you to attack those creatures, so the cross had no reason to obey your command to attack. You weren't in any immediate danger, and you weren't in need of being protected. Do you understand?"

"Yeah, I think so. It's kind of like I shouldn't fight unless there's no other choice, right?"

"Something like that," Mike said with a smile. "So what else did you learn from observing this species?"

"Well, it's like they were the exact opposite of those on the last planet you took me to. On the previous planet, everyone seemed to be connected with pure love. On this planet, everyone seems to be connected with pure hate. On the other planet, they admired the cross and the name of Jesus, but on this planet, they despise those same things and what they stand for. It's confusing how two planets and two races of people can receive the same message and go in such opposite directions. Everyone on the last planet was so happy and at peace, but everyone here is so evil and vicious— everyone except for Sitrof, that is. He said that out of the whole planet, less than forty of them still believe in Jesus's message.

Maybe he can someday raise that number and make a difference in this world," Christopher said.

"Unfortunately, I think that is going to be awfully hard for Sitrof to do," Mike said.

"What do you mean?"

"Never mind, Chris. You said you are ready to go home, didn't you? It doesn't matter."

"What doesn't matter, Mike? Now, quit playin', and tell me what you meant."

"Sitrof was captured by Mandar and his men. He will be put to death within the hour. I'm sorry. There's nothing you could have done."

"No! Not Sitrof! He doesn't deserve to die. Man, see? I knew it. If the cross would have just let me attack them in the building, Sitrof would have had more time to get away," Christopher said angrily.

"That's not your choice to make, Chris. We cannot do something we know is wrong, even if it is in the hopes that we will prevent a future wrong."

"Why not? Why should a being as evil as Mandar get to live while a being as good as Sitrof has to die? How is that fair?"

"Life isn't about what's fair, Christopher. God gave all of his creations free will. As a consequence of that gift, things are not always fair. Sitrof knew that, which is why he knew the danger he would always face on this planet. The difference between good and evil lies in the choices we make and the actions we take."

Christopher stood there shaking his head, trying to process everything Mike had just explained to him. He could think only about how a good person like Sitrof didn't deserve to die at the hands of a ruthless dictator like Mandar.

Mike studied Christopher as he paced back and forth, reading Christopher's thoughts. In response to one thought, he immediately said, "Don't even think about that, Chris."

"Why not? You said the difference between good and evil is in the choices we make and the actions we take. I've made my choice. I'm going to help Sitrof!"

"You can't, Chris. There are three of them, and you cannot possibly fight all three of them. Even if you could, by now, Mandar has probably already assembled other members of his regime to witness the execution. Remember, you cannot use the power of the cross to attack, even if what you want to attack is evil."

"That's fine. Then I won't use it to attack. I'll just use it to protect Sitrof. You said yourself that the power can be used for protection. Well, Sitrof needs protection now. I'm going to help him. Now, please tell me where they are, Mike! Please help me save him!"

"You understand that I cannot follow you once again, right? You will be on your own without a guide."

"That's fine. Just tell me where they are."

"Christopher, you must understand that this is for real. You can be killed and die on this planet. Your family and friends would never know what happened to you. Furthermore, even if you are somehow able to save Sitrof today, he could very well be killed tomorrow. That is the way life is on this planet."

"I understand that, but tomorrow it won't be my fault that he was captured. The only reason they found Sitrof today was because they were looking for me. I can't be the reason he gets murdered. Now, please, time is wasting. Help me do the right thing, and tell me where they are."

Mike stood there in thought. He was determining the exact location of Sitrof and his captors. He looked at Christopher, pointed his finger, and said, "They are a mile that way, but you won't make it in time. You can't possibly run that fast and fight through all the dangers on the way."

"I have to try, Mike!"

"I know, which is why I will transport you there. Just please make sure this is really what you want before I do. There will be no turning back."

"I'm sure."

"I know you are, but I had to hear you say it. Good luck, and may God bless you and protect you."

"Thank you, Mike. If I don't make it, thank you for everything you have shown me. I finally understand," Christopher said.

Mike closed his eyes, and Christopher disappeared in front of him. Mike looked up at the sky, into the heavens above, and said with a smile, "As usual, you were right about him, Lord. He is special."

CHAPTER 8

The Battle

C HRISTOPHER SUDDENLY APPEARED
out of nowhere, transported by the crystal, standing next to an enormous tree that had been split in half right down the middle. The rest of the surrounding area was nothing but open space all around, except for a large hill about two hundred yards directly to the right. Christopher was only twenty feet behind Sitrof and his evil captors. They had not seen Christopher get transported, nor did they see him standing behind them.

Mandar stood in the middle, with Allanac to his right and Tadlos to his left. Sitrof was on his knees in front of them, with the black ocean crashing its thunderous waves down behind him. Christopher's heart sank as he saw that the friendly and good-hearted Sitrof appeared to have been badly beaten; he had bruises and cuts all over his face and body.

Christopher started walking up slowly behind them. He pulled his cross out of the right pocket of his jeans to have it ready when needed. He tried to plan his attack as he listened to Mandar talk. The menacing dictator was yelling, which Christopher found strange, considering Sitrof was on his knees only a foot in front of him. Then

Christopher felt his stomach turn as he saw something that made him feel ill: standing along the hill were at least two hundred of Mandar's soldiers and followers. They were there to watch their leader finally murder the notorious Sitrof. It was a proud moment for Mandar to finally remove the thorn that had been in his side for years. Mandar wanted to show his followers that no one could escape his wrath. No matter how many times Sitrof had escaped, it had been inevitable that Mandar would catch up with him, and it was now his time.

Christopher wondered how he was going to save his new friend now. He had worried about taking on just three of the mighty alien warriors earlier, but now a whole army had arrived to witness their leader strike down yet another enemy.

"Sitrof, you have been a worthy adversary over the years, but your luck has finally run out. Do you have any last words before being put to death?" Mandar said.

Sitrof said, "Forgive them, Lord, for they know not what they do."

Mandar punched Sitrof in the mouth, angry that his last words had referenced the Lord. Sitrof fell back and lay flat on the ground. Allanac and Tadlos took turns kicking him in the ribs and stomach, with each kick adding more damage to the beating he had already taken. Mandar smiled at the look of pain on Sitrof's face. With each kick, the crowd of Mandar's followers roared and cheered louder and louder.

"Enough," Mandar said finally, and the crowd became silent. "It's time to finish this. Tadlos, hold him steady."

Mandar pulled his mighty sword out of its sheath and held it up over his head for his followers to both admire and fear. He then placed the mighty blade against Sitrof's neck. "Goodbye, Sitrof. Too bad you would not join me when you had the chance." Mandar pulled back his sword to get full momentum and finish Sitrof with a single swing.

"No!" Christopher yelled out in fear. He instinctively held out his crystal cross, and a ray of pure light and power shot out of it and hit Mandar's sword, knocking it out of the giant warrior's hand. The sword spiraled through the air and landed at least twenty feet from its owner.

Sitrof saw Christopher standing there, and an enormous smile came over his face.

"That's the puny creature and his weapon? Get him! Get him, and bring him to me now," Mandar commanded. He signaled for all his troops standing on the hill to wait, as he had no doubt that he and his two best soldiers could take out Sitrof and Christopher. After giving the signal, he turned around slowly and went to pick up his sword.

Tadlos and Allanac ran toward Christopher. Sitrof, using the last bit of energy he had, reached out and grabbed Allanac by the ankle, tripping him. Allanac fell to the ground. Tadlos continued running at Christopher at full speed.

Christopher stood firm, waiting for Tadlos's charge. Tadlos yelled, "You won't be so lucky this time, weird creature! This time, I will kill you!"

Christopher moved to his right, and the less-agile creature ran right past him. As Tadlos passed him, Christopher stuck out his foot and swept Tadlos down to the ground, where he landed face-first. Tadlos quickly got up, now even angrier. Tadlos again ran toward Christopher. Christopher held out his cross, and Tadlos came to a sudden halt. The creature stood there staring at the cross, remembering the last time he had seen it. A feeling he had never known in battle before came over him: the feeling of pure fear. He feared Mandar, but he had never had a fear of being defeated in a battle before. He'd thought that was one of the benefits of joining Mandar: he would never have to taste defeat.

"What's the matter? Is the big, tough soldier afraid of a little crystal?" Christopher said, taunting him.

Tadlos grew enraged, as he was not one to be criticized and

played with. He howled and continued his charge at Christopher, even more determined.

The crystal began to glow, and a ray of light streamed out from it. The light hit Tadlos right in the chest. Tadlos braced for the impact this time, but it still knocked him back ten to fifteen feet and brought him down to his knees. However, Tadlos was a strong warrior and was not about to give up. He struggled back to his feet and again charged at Christopher.

The cross shot another ray at Tadlos. This time, it was a full-force shot. It hit Tadlos right in the chest again. Even though Tadlos once again braced for the impact, the force of the light picked him up and threw him at least three hundred yards through the air, out past the hill and the battalion of soldiers. The soldiers watched one of their leaders fly past them overhead, not knowing what to make of what they were seeing. Finally, the light dimmed, and Tadlos dropped to the ground as Mandar's followers watched in amazement. They couldn't believe what had just happened to one of their fiercest warriors. Tadlos had been defeated, knocked out, and maybe humbled by the power of the cross.

Christopher turned back around to see Allanac and Sitrof rolling on the ground, trading punches with each other. Sitrof was beaten and weak but was still able to hold his own against Allanac. He felt rejuvenated after seeing Christopher and his cross come to his rescue, knowing that Christopher, a stranger from another planet, had risked life and death to save him. It gave him the strength he needed to want to fight on. He knew that one person could make a difference.

In the meantime, Mandar had picked up his deadly sword and witnessed his number-one soldier be defeated by the small piece of crystal. He walked with great determination toward the cross and its owner.

Christopher saw Mandar coming toward him, and what a menacing and intimidating sight he was. It was no wonder he was a feared leader on that planet. He was a frightening being who showed no fear, weakness, or mercy. Christopher knew that to truly save Sitrof, he would have to defeat Mandar.

With Mandar walking toward him, Christopher walked toward Mandar. Mandar raised his arm to signal his troops to come down the hill. Christopher became frightened, for not only was he about to battle the undefeated Mandar, but now an alien army was coming down the hill toward him. He wasn't sure if Mandar had signaled for them to simply come down and watch from a closer vantage point or if they were coming to join in on the kill. They ran down the sloping hill, and Christopher could only imagine what horrible ending he and Sitrof were about to suffer.

The sound of a thousand footsteps charging all at once sounded like an out-of-control freight train coming toward Christopher. He turned to see the massive cloud of red dust being kicked up by the warriors running toward him at full speed. Then, all on its own, the crystal cross lit up and projected a wave of light that rushed toward the oncoming soldiers. The wave of light, upon reaching the charging aliens, became a giant wall of protection that the soldiers could not get through. They took turns trying to run through the wall of light—punching it, kicking it, and slicing at it with their swords—but it was no use. Nothing they did could break the force field provided by the cross, and the soldiers could not get through or around the great barrier. No matter how determined they were to follow Mandar's orders, the army of killers were going to be nothing more than spectators and could not interfere.

Mandar looked on, shocked at what had just happened. The small cross held by the inferior human had defeated his number-one soldier and rendered his army useless. He was aggravated beyond belief, yet he was intrigued by the power of the cross. He now had a dual motive to strike down Christopher: to defeat an opponent and to capture the cross and control the power it possessed.

Mandar continued walking and came within striking distance of Christopher. He raised his sword and swung it with the intention of defeating the small human with a single swipe of his razor-sharp saber.

Christopher held out his cross, and once again, a ray of light shot out of it. The ray hit Mandar's sword. Mandar watched his sword fly off into the distance, this time even farther out of his reach. Mandar turned back to look at Christopher and said with his deep, menacing voice, "I do not need my sword to defeat such a lesser being. You are an insect and not worthy enough to have the honor of being put to death by my sword. I will kill you with my own bare hands, breaking one bone at a time as you scream out in pain."

The crowd of soldiers cheered at their leader's words.

Mandar drew back his arm to swing at Christopher. Christopher held out his cross so that it could send Mandar flying away, as it had done to Tadlos. He waited for the glow to fill the crystal, but once again, nothing happened. It was just like when he had tried to use it in the abandoned building. Christopher realized the cross was not responding, but it was too late now, as Mandar's punch was about to connect with him.

Christopher had just enough time to instinctively try to roll with the punch to avoid any damage. The punch from the vicious warrior hit Christopher in the back of his shoulder blade and sent him flying through the air. He landed stomach first on the ground, kicking up a massive amount of the red dust as he skidded to a stop. Mandar let out an evil laugh as he watched the small creature slam into the ground. The crowd once again roared louder than before.

Christopher looked at his cross, which had fallen out of his hand and landed a few yards in front of him. "Why won't you work now? I wasn't attacking; I was being attacked," he said to the cross.

Christopher struggled to his feet just in time for Mandar to grab him from behind. Mandar picked up the small human and, with one hand, held Christopher over his head. He then threw Christopher the way a child might have thrown a doll. Christopher landed on his back, once again kicking up dust and gravel when he hit the ground. He looked at his cross in desperation.

"If you won't attack for me, at least give me the strength to fight this creature!" Christopher pleaded.

At that moment, the cross lit up with a glow that illuminated the entire surrounding area. A ray of light shot out of the crystal cross and hit Christopher right in the heart. The light surrounded him, and at first, he thought he was going to be punished for making the request. Then he realized the cross was granting his wish. It was filling him with the power and strength necessary to make the fight with the much larger alien fair.

The light dimmed, and the glow from the cross once again distinguished, having fulfilled its duty.

Mandar stood there looking at Christopher, confused as to what had just happened. Christopher went down to one knee after receiving the light from the cross. He looked at the cross and said thank you. He felt a strength within him that he had never felt before. He said, "Thank you, Lord."

Hearing those words infuriated Mandar, who charged at Christopher to inflict more punishment on him. Christopher stood there waiting for the charge. When Mandar was close enough and about to throw a punch, Christopher cocked back his arm and punched Mandar in the center of the chest. Mandar went flying backward through the air and landed on his back. This time, it was his body that hit the ground and kicked up dust—something the gigantic warrior had never experienced before.

The roaring from the crowd of soldiers suddenly stopped, and they all gasped in shock upon seeing their leader and general lying on his back. Mandar had never been knocked down in a battle before. In fact, he had never even come close to being knocked onto his back. He did not like the feeling, but unlike Tadlos, he did not have a feeling of fear. He became even angrier and more enraged, furious with himself for allowing the tiny, unworthy human to knock him down. He also was angry that his army had witnessed the event, as he knew that scene could lead to some of them challenging him in the future. He was going to really have to make Christopher pay now.

Mandar stood up and, with an evil smirk, brushed the red gravel from his body. "Maybe I misjudged you, small one. Maybe you are a worthy adversary to battle against—or maybe you just got a lucky punch in. Nevertheless, the outcome will still be the same. You cannot and will not defeat me."

"Well, come on with it then," Christopher replied, trying to hide his fear and portray a hint of confidence.

Mandar walked up to Christopher, and the two foes stood there circling each other. Each fighter was looking for an opening that would give him the upper hand. It was a true case of David versus Goliath. On one side was Christopher, who was only five foot nine, and on the other side was Mandar, a towering eight feet of solid muscle. Mandar was a natural-born killer. Christopher knew that he was still faster than Mandar, and the cross had evened out the great disparity in their strength. However, Mandar was obviously much more experienced in life-or-death combat and had never lost such a battle.

Off in the distance, Sitrof and Allanac were still battling as well. Sitrof was injured and tired but would not give in to defeat. Allanac landed a punch to Sitrof's head that knocked him back to the ground. Allanac immediately jumped on top of Sitrof to keep dishing out punishment. He threw another punch to Sitrof's jaw, nearly knocking him unconscious. Allanac then flipped Sitrof over onto his stomach, knelt on his back, and put him in a headlock. He then held Sitrof's head up so that Sitrof could see Christopher and Mandar do battle.

"Look over there, Sitrof. Watch as Mandar is about to pummel your puny ally to a pulp. Once I finish you off, I will go over there to help my master destroy your friend."

"Please, Jesus, give me strength," Sitrof whispered.

Just then, Sitrof summoned every last ounce of energy in his body and threw a vicious elbow to the eye on the right side of Allanac's head. Allanac fell off of Sitrof, grabbing his eye in pain. Sitrof climbed to his feet and grabbed Allanac by his hair. He punched Allanac in the face repeatedly until he couldn't punch anymore. He let go of Allanac, who slithered to the ground like a bowl of Jell-O and passed out, defeated.

"Okay, Chris, now it's definitely a one-on-one fight between you and Mandar. You can do it. Take it to him," Sitrof whispered. With that, his legs buckled, and he too fell to the ground, completely exhausted.

Mandar and Christopher were still circling each other, both moving slowly in a clockwise circle. The sound of thunder erupted all around them as each wave from the black ocean crashed down. Christopher knew better than to be the one to initiate contact. He would wait for Mandar to throw a punch, and then he would try to counterpunch. With the speed advantage he held, he figured that would be his best way to attack. As in football and basketball, he knew that sometimes the best offense was a good defense.

Mandar sized up his opponent, looking for Christopher's weak spots. Mandar noticed that the smaller creature seemed to have good balance, and he also knew the human was faster than he was. However, he knew that if he could knock Christopher off balance to get him on the ground, the fight would be over. His height and longer reach were huge advantages. He knew his experience was far greater, and he had an unwavering confidence and arrogance about him. Mandar looked off into the distance with his side eye and saw Sitrof and Allanac lying on the ground.

"Looks like Sitrof will not be able to come save you, little one," Mandar said to Christopher, hoping to discourage him.

"Funny. I was thinking about how Allanac wouldn't be able to come save you," Christopher said. He knew it was important not to let Mandar see how afraid he was.

"I don't need anyone to finish off an inferior little believer like you."

With that, Mandar swung his massive, muscular right arm at Christopher's head. Christopher instinctively ducked the punch and threw his own right-handed uppercut directly into Mandar's rib cage. Mandar bent over, grabbing his ribs in pain after the powerful blow from the small human. By bending over, Mandar inadvertently shrank himself to Christopher's height. Christopher threw another punch, this time an overhanded left. His fist connected with the side of Mandar's head, and the crushing punch sent Mandar to his knees.

Seeing Mandar on his knees, Christopher moved in farther with his attack. Mandar saw it coming and backhanded Christopher across the face with his massive right hand. Christopher stumbled back, worried about what damage the punch might have done to him. However, he realized that when the cross had given him the same strength as Mandar, it also had given him the same stamina and ability to take a punch. The power of the cross truly had evened the playing field and given Christopher a real chance to win.

Mandar got back up and ran at Christopher like a bull charging a matador. He threw a massive left-handed punch toward Christopher's head. Christopher once again ducked and was about to throw another punch to Mandar's ribs; however, the experienced warrior saw that Christopher was about to make the mistake of executing the same maneuver again. When Christopher threw his punch, Mandar quickly spun around to catch it. Mandar grabbed Christopher's right arm and threw him the way an Olympic athlete would have thrown a discus.

Christopher went spiraling through the air like a boomerang. He landed hard on his stomach with a thud. It was a quick lesson for Christopher to remember. He was still heavily outweighed by his enormous opponent. Mandar could still throw him like a doll if he got Christopher in his grasp. Christopher had to remember to be patient and use his speed to win the fight.

Mandar quickly maneuvered over to where Christopher had landed. Christopher quickly got up and stood there waiting for the giant to arrive. Mandar drew his right arm back to throw a punch, but this time, Christopher wasn't going to wait for it to arrive. He quickly threw a left-handed jab to Mandar's chest, catching the bigger creature off guard. Mandar stepped back, and Christopher threw five more combination punches to Mandar's chest and stomach area. Each punch knocked Mandar a little farther back. Mandar was caught off guard by Christopher's aggressive attack. Christopher then took a step back, as he didn't want to stand toe to toe with that creature, trading punches.

Mandar regained his composure and stood there smiling at Christopher. "Nice little barrage of punches you threw there. But you are going to have to do a lot more than that to actually hurt me."

"Thanks for the tip, but tell me if this hurts," Christopher said as he faked a punch to Mandar's chest. When Mandar moved to block the punch, Christopher kicked him on the side of his knee.

Mandar let out a moan of pain and dropped down to his other knee, once again making himself the same height as Christopher. Christopher threw an uppercut right to Mandar's jaw that sent him flying into the air. Christopher stood there in shock, watching the eight-foot-tall red giant fly through the yellow sky. Mandar landed face-first on the red ground. The impact made such a thud that Christopher wasn't sure if the sound was the impact of Mandar hitting the ground or another wave from the black ocean crashing down.

The crowd of soldiers watched in disbelief as the mighty Mandar was knocked down again. Unbelievably, Mandar got right back to his feet without any hesitation. "That hurt a little, but it still isn't enough to even come close to stopping me," Mandar said as he again walked toward Christopher with an evil grin on his face.

Christopher was now more afraid than he had been before. He had landed a perfect combination attack against the alien creature, and the attack hadn't seemed to slow Mandar down for more than a moment. Christopher had thought he was winning the fight punch for punch at that point, yet Mandar was still coming after him. In any other fight Christopher had been in, an attack like that would have ended the fight, but against Mandar, it seemed to be nothing more than a slap to the face. Mandar was like a machine fueled by pure hatred. The more he was hurt, the angrier and more filled with energy he became.

Christopher didn't have the luxury of being afraid. There was too much at stake—both his own life and Sitrof's. He realized he was thinking too much. The more one thought in a fight, the more dangerous the situation became. A fighter could not allow himself to think of the outcome of a fight or worry about the aftermath. Christopher had to concentrate on staying in the moment. He had to trust his instincts, stop thinking, and just react. He'd let the fight come to him, he thought. He put his guard up and walked toward Mandar.

The two fighters circled each other again. Christopher didn't know it, but Mandar was starting to see the fear in the small human. At the same time, he was also gaining a small amount of respect for him. That respect wouldn't stop him from killing Christopher, of course, but Mandar felt that Christopher would be a good and worthy kill. The fact that the puny and weak creature had put up that much of a fight was a shock to Mandar. Mandar usually had already destroyed his opponents by then. However, he had been unable to get in a good hit that caused any real damage so far. He knew his performance had changed his army's perception of him and the battle. Christopher had gone from being a joke of an opponent and an easy victory to a formidable alien warrior with lightning-quick reflexes, deceptive speed, and a powerful weapon in the cross.

Mandar would no longer be ridiculed for taking so long to finish off his enemy; rather, he would be celebrated for defeating a believer from another world. His victory would cement his legacy and prove that no believer, no matter what world he was from, was more powerful than he was.

The fighters circled one another, waiting for the perfect moment to attack. Christopher glanced past Mandar and saw Sitrof still lying on the ground, passed out from exhaustion. Mandar saw Christopher's momentary glance toward Sitrof and threw down a right-handed punch toward Christopher's head. Christopher was able to regain his focus, and with his superior speed, he dodged the slower Mandar's punch by moving to the left. Mandar, quick to recover from a missed shot, backhanded Christopher across the face with the same hand. Christopher fell back only a few feet from the force of the muscular backhand, but while off balance, he lost his footing on the gravel-like soil and fell to the ground.

Christopher shook off the right-handed slap, but this time, Mandar was determined to take advantage of the fact that Christopher was on the ground. Christopher looked up as Mandar flew through the air, about to pounce right on top of him.

Christopher quickly extended both legs upward, and his feet caught Mandar in midair. He then used Mandar's leaping momentum to catapult the giant over his head. Mandar landed awkwardly and skidded across the dirt, kicking up a huge amount of red dust. Christopher then jumped up from the ground and ran toward Mandar to take advantage of the taller creature's position on the ground.

Christopher ran full speed into the cloud of red dust that lingered where Mandar had landed. There was so much dust that Christopher seemed to disappear into it for a moment. Then, just as quickly as he had run into the dust storm, Christopher was thrown back out of it. Mandar had known that Christopher would charge him, and he had used the dust to disguise his attack. Christopher had run full speed right into Mandar's waiting fist.

The young human flew at least twenty-five feet through the air and crashed into the trunk of the broken old tree split down the middle. He bounced off the tree and landed directly on his back. He seemed to be hurt for the first time, and he lay there next to the tree, wincing in pain and grabbing his lower back. Since he hadn't seen the blow from Mandar coming, he'd had no time to brace for the impact. After the punch and the impact with the tree, Christopher was shaken up.

Mandar quickly followed Christopher out of the cloud of dust, which was starting to settle back to the ground. He spotted Christopher lying there in pain and ran over to him, hoping to finish off his kill.

Christopher saw Mandar coming toward him and tried to get up, but he couldn't. He was still rattled and unsteady from the blind attack Mandar had thrust upon him. Mandar was now only ten feet away. Christopher dug his hands into the red gravel and gave another push to try to get up. He was still too dazed and disoriented to succeed in rising to his feet.

Mandar was now only five feet away. Christopher knew he was in trouble. If Mandar got to him while he was still on the ground, Mandar would win the battle and finish him for sure. Christopher knew he could not compete in a wrestling match with a being of Mandar's size, skill, and strength. All the advantages Christopher possessed—speed, agility, balance—would have been nullified.

Mandar was now only a foot away from Christopher, and he reached his enormous hand out to grab him.

Christopher grabbed a handful of the gravel-like red soil and threw it directly into Mandar's eyes. Mandar grabbed his eyes with both hands, trying desperately to flush the dust and dirt out of them. That street-fighter move bought Christopher the time he needed, and he was finally able to get to his feet. Next to him on the ground was a huge branch that had fallen off the broken tree when he slammed into it. The branch was at least six feet long and probably weighed close to two hundred pounds. Christopher picked up the huge branch as if it were just a large baseball bat. If not for the increased strength he had received from the cross, he would never have been able to lift the fallen tree limb so easily.

Christopher walked up behind Mandar and swung the gigantic club, hitting Mandar square in the center of the back. Mandar fell a few feet forward. Christopher knew he had to be careful. Mandar had eyes on either side of his head, so the gravel Christopher had thrown had not completely blinded him.

As Mandar continued to try to get his eyes cleared up, Christopher again hit him with the large branch, this time in the stomach area. Christopher made a conscious effort to stay either directly in front of or directly behind Mandar. That way, the eyes on the sides of Mandar's head could not aid him.

Mandar groaned in pain and frustration after the second hit with the enormous branch. The soldiers were still watching intently and couldn't believe the fight they were witnessing.

Mandar's vision had now all but cleared up. He blinked repeatedly to see what was in front of him, but he did not see Christopher. He turned around quickly, sensing that Christopher must have been behind him, but it was too late. As Mandar turned around, Christopher was already in full swing, wielding his branch like a golf club this time. The mighty swing caught Mandar right underneath the chin, sending him airborne through the yellow sky.

Christopher stood there watching Mandar fly through the air the way a baseball player watched a home run fly out of a ballpark. Mandar must have landed at least sixty feet from where Christopher was standing. Mandar tried to get up, but this time, he was too disoriented to stand on his own feet. Once again, he had never known that feeling in battle. He had never been almost knocked unconscious before.

Mandar saw Christopher moving toward him and realized the fortunes had switched. Just a few moments ago, he had been moving in for the kill on Christopher. Now Christopher was moving in to finish him off. Mandar looked around frantically for something to help him get to his feet, but there was nothing but open land around him. There was nothing to lean on or pull himself up with. Then Mandar saw something only a few feet from him that filled his face with an evil, spine-tingling smirk. He crawled on his stomach toward it.

Christopher was almost to Mandar now. Mandar continued his belly crawl toward his new goal. Christopher saw Mandar crawling but could not see what he was crawling for. He assumed Mandar was just trying to get away from him and buy time to recover from the strikes Christopher had delivered.

Mandar finally reached what he had been crawling toward and wrapped his hand around it. Christopher still could not see it, as Mandar's herculean body blocked his view. What was it that Mandar had been crawling toward? What was the thing he had seen that had given him renewed confidence that he could now end and win the fight? Mandar had found his mighty sword.

Mandar had flown so far through the air that he had landed right next to the sword he had lost earlier in the fight. The mighty sword he had used to strike down so many previous opponents was back in his possession. It was a different game now. Now all Mandar had to do was wait patiently for Christopher to come a little closer, and then he could attack with the sharp and deadly blade.

"Mandar, give up now, and you can walk away with your pride.

I don't want to hurt you anymore. We can call this a draw and both come out winners!" Christopher yelled to him.

"That's the problem with you believers: you don't have the guts to finish what you start. You are all pathetic and weak," Mandar replied.

"It's called mercy, Mandar, and it's what separates people like me and Sitrof from people like you."

"Really? I thought what separated us was the fact that I kill people like you."

Off in the distance, Sitrof was regaining consciousness. He glanced up and saw Mandar lying on the ground with Christopher walking up next to him. Sitrof gave a brief smile that soon turned to a look of concern. Sitrof was able to see that Mandar was holding his sword and that Christopher was unaware of it. He also noticed that they were talking, which meant Mandar was purposely stalling and trying to get Christopher to drop his guard. He was planning to attack when Christopher least expected it.

"Chris, watch out!" Sitrof yelled. But it was no use. Christopher could not hear him over the deafening waves of the black ocean smacking down behind him.

"Mandar, you lost. I could have finished you off by now and ended your life, but I haven't. I'm not a murderer like you. Leave now, and let this be the end of it," Christopher said.

"You know what your problem is, believer? You talk too much." With that, Mandar jumped to his feet and, in one fluid motion, swung his sword around to try to stab Christopher.

Christopher was startled, but luckily, he inadvertently blocked the swing of the sword with his bat-like branch. The sword cut through the branch like a machete cutting through a head of lettuce. Still, the branch slowed the momentum of the sword just enough for Christopher to jump back out of the reach of the blade.

Mandar moved slowly closer to Christopher. He moved the way a predator moved when it had its prey cornered.

"What was that you were saying to me, you little rodent? Oh, that's right. I believe you said I had lost. I am Mandar! I don't lose!" Mandar shouted with conviction and authority. He raised the massive sword above his head and swung the mighty blade down, aiming right at Christopher's head.

Christopher somersaulted out of the way at the last minute, just as the sword reached where his head would have been. After rising from his somersault on the ground, Christopher was able to kick the sword from Mandar's giant hand. However, Mandar then spun, kicked his right leg, and caught Christopher with a clean shot to the back of the head. The kick from the muscular alien's leg knocked Christopher off his feet and back down to the dirt. Then the thing Christopher had most tried to prevent in the fight happened: Mandar jumped on top of him.

Mandar knelt on top of Christopher, throwing punch after punch to Christopher's ribs and stomach. Christopher tried to counterpunch, but Mandar seemed more than willing to trade punches from that angle. Christopher struggled to break free, but it was no use. Mandar landed a right hook to Christopher's eye that cut Christopher badly. Christopher felt beyond weakened after the crushing blow. Mandar continued landing his barrage of punches to Christopher's face and body and then started shaking and thrashing Christopher around the way a shark thrashed its prey. Christopher's head bounced off the gravel repeatedly as Mandar shook his body, lifting him up and then driving him into the ground with his full body weight.

Christopher was barely able to see straight and was severely wounded by the attack. Mandar finally stopped throwing punches and stood up over him. Christopher was barely conscious by that time. He had multiple cuts, his eye was swollen and beginning to shut, and he was already bruising. He tried to focus his eyes, but his vision was so blurred that he saw three of Mandar.

Mandar then said, "You have fought valiantly, little one, but no one can defeat Mandar. Especially some alien boy who carries around a cross for protection." He grabbed Christopher with one hand by his shirt and lifted him off the ground. He made Christopher stand up on his wobbly legs, even though he could barely keep his balance.

Mandar picked up his sword and spoke in an arrogant tone of voice. "Goodbye, believer. Now you can see if you are able to meet your silly God face-to-face." He reared back his sword with both hands to deliver the kill shot to Christopher's torso.

Christopher saw the sword coming, but he was so weak he couldn't move out of the way of it. It was about to stab right through his midsection, and even though his brain was telling him to move, his body wouldn't respond. Christopher saw visions of his family and friends flash before his eyes, especially images of his mom and dad and Joey. He saw all the good memories they had given him throughout his life, as if he were watching a movie. He was going to miss them all so much. *Do they even know how much I love them and how much they mean to me?* he wondered.

All of a sudden, as Mandar's blade was about to strike Christopher down for good, Sitrof pushed Christopher out of the way and jumped in front of the mighty sword. The blade went right through Sitrof's body and through his muscular back.

"No!" Christopher shouted as he saw Sitrof take the blade in order to save his life. Christopher got up and stood there in disbelief.

Mandar was standing there with a great sense of pride and achievement. While he hadn't killed his intended target, he had finally run his sword through his elusive enemy, Sitrof. The crowd of a thousand soldiers went crazy, jumping up and down and cheering at the sight of Mandar's sword slicing through Sitrof. Mandar then lifted Sitrof up and threw his limp body toward the black ocean. Sitrof landed near the shore and did not move. He was dying, for the wound he had suffered was a mortal one.

Christopher tried to run over to his friend, but Mandar stood in his way with his deadly sword in hand. Mandar turned his head, looked at Sitrof lying there motionless, and said, "How unfortunate, Sitrof. You gave your worthy life to save this creature, and now he will meet the same fate as you."

Christopher saw a big rock lying on the ground next to his foot. He picked it up like a football, drew his arm back, and threw it as hard as he could. It was the most perfect pass of his life. The rock darted through the air and crashed right into Mandar's head, cutting the back of his skull. Mandar grabbed his head in pain, shocked to discover that he was now the one bleeding. Christopher felt a rush of adrenaline shoot through his body after witnessing his friend's sacrifice. He realized the rock he had thrown had hurt Mandar, who was stumbling. He ran at Mandar full speed.

Mandar saw him coming but was still hurt and dizzy. He swung his sword at Christopher's head—more to keep Christopher at a distance than to strike him. Christopher ducked the swing of the sword and came up with an uppercut punch right to Mandar's groin area. Mandar dropped his sword and grabbed his groin with both hands as he roared in pain.

"I guess that hurts just as much on this planet as it does on mine, huh?" Christopher said.

Christopher then picked up the rock he had thrown at Mandar and hit Mandar over the head with it. Mandar went right down to the ground in pain. Christopher knelt down, putting his knee into Mandar's throat. He then grabbed Mandar by his hair and punched him as hard as he could right on his chiseled jaw. Time after time, Christopher hit him, until finally, Mandar was bruised and unconscious on the ground.

The mighty Mandar had been defeated and lay there as still as a log.

Christopher stepped back and picked up Mandar's sword. The amazing blade was nearly as long as Christopher was. *What a fitting death it would be for Mandar to die by the same sword that has killed so many,* Christopher thought. He raised the mighty sword above his head, ready to stab the unknowing Mandar.

Christopher wanted to do it—he felt Mandar deserved it—but he couldn't. He couldn't kill him, for he knew that if he did, he was no better than Mandar was. A thought came to his mind. It was one of Jesus's teachings: *"Those who live by the sword, die by the sword."* Christopher knew he couldn't use Mandar's sword, or he might become like Mandar. Instead, he turned and threw the mighty sword with all his strength. It flew through the sky blade over hilt and landed far into the black ocean. Christopher then turned and ran over to his friend Sitrof, who was lying there without life.

CHAPTER 9

Rebirth

CHRISTOPHER KNELT DOWN BESIDE HIS giant friend who had sacrificed his life to protect him. He gently placed his hand underneath Sitrof's head. "Sitrof! Sitrof, can you hear me? Come on, Sitrof. It's not time for you to die yet. You can't be dead. Come on. Get up."

It was no use; Sitrof couldn't respond.

"I was supposed to save you! You weren't supposed to die saving me! I'm so sorry, Sitrof," Christopher said with a tear rolling down his cheek. "I'm so sorry I couldn't save you. Even though I just met you, there was something special about you. This world needs good men like you. Men who are willing to stand up for what they believe in. Men who will stand up against the evils of this world. Please forgive me for failing."

Off in the distance, Mandar was waking up. He was shaken up from the beating he had just taken. He had never been knocked down in a fight, let alone knocked completely unconscious in one. It was a new experience for him, and he wasn't sure how to feel. He tried to get up but could barely lift his head off the ground. He grabbed his head, trying to make the pounding pain stop. He was lightheaded and dizzy, but he finally was able to sit up enough to look up and see Christopher. He saw the human sitting there on the ground, holding the dead Sitrof in his arms. A smile came over Mandar's face, as if he took pleasure in seeing the grief Christopher was feeling. He sat up completely, trying to remain quiet. He hoped to regain his energy, and maybe in a few minutes, he could attack Christopher from behind while he was grieving.

Christopher held Sitrof's massive head against his chest. "God, why did he have to die? He believed in you. In a place where people aren't supposed to believe in you, where they are murdered for believing in you, he still did! He still chose to! I wish he were still alive." Another tear slid slowly down his face.

All of a sudden, Christopher felt something happening to his left. He glanced over and saw his crystal cross glowing. The light was both beautiful and blinding. Then the light turned into a solid stream that shot out from the cross directly into the lifeless Sitrof. The surge of light slamming into Sitrof jolted Christopher and pushed him back a few feet. The mesmerizing light engulfed Sitrof's whole body until his shape could no longer be seen. There was a cocoon of brightness around him. Christopher looked on with confusion and amazement.

Oddly, off in the distance, Mandar watched with the same feelings. Neither of the adversaries knew what was happening inside the cocoon of light.

The light from the crystal cross dimmed, and the cocoon of light around Sitrof slowly extinguished. Christopher saw his friend lying there again, but then something amazing happened.

Sitrof sat up. He had a smile on his face that seemed to be glowing. He looked over at Christopher and nodded at him with pure joy.

"Sitrof, you're alive!" Christopher shouted ecstatically, astonished.

Mandar couldn't believe his eyes. He became filled with anger upon seeing his longtime enemy he finally had struck down suddenly come back to life. "What kind of magic is that little cross filled with?" Mandar said to himself.

"Sitrof, are you okay? Do you feel all right?" Christopher asked while helping Sitrof to his feet.

"Yes, Christopher. I've never felt better in my entire life. Thank you, God. Thank you, Jesus," the born-again Sitrof said. "And thank you, Christopher. Thank you for saving me."

"I didn't do anything, Sitrof. You jumped in front of Mandar's sword to save me, and you died. But the cross brought you back to life. I can't take credit for any of it," Christopher said.

"You did save me. First, you came to my aid when I was about to be killed by Mandar and his two soldiers. Then I saw Mandar about to run you through with his sword, so I had to return the favor and try to save you. Without hesitation or thinking, I just did what I knew I had to do. Yes, I died in trying to do that, but your faith and compassion helped bring me back to life."

"Well, I'm just happy you're alive. I still can't believe it. Like you just said, thank you, God, and thank you, Jesus. That is all I can say." Christopher hugged his giant friend.

Sitrof smiled as he hugged Christopher back. Rarely had Sitrof felt such a tender moment. On that planet, such a sign of joy and true happiness was rarely exhibited. Sitrof relished and cherished the feeling.

Mandar watched the events unfold in front of him in disbelief. He despised the moment. He had to make it stop, and he saw his opportunity to make it end permanently.

Christopher and Sitrof let go of their embrace, and Sitrof said, "Your kind certainly heal fast, don't they? You no longer have any visible injuries on you after your battle with Mandar."

Christopher felt his face and looked down at his hands. Sitrof was correct: there was not a single mark on him. His eye was no longer swollen; there were no longer any cuts on his face from all the punches Mandar had hit him with. There were no longer any marks on his hands or knuckles where he had landed punches. Then he realized that before the light had surrounded Sitrof to revive him, it first had hit Christopher, knocking him back. That little bit of light from the cross had healed him of all the scrapes and bruises he had endured.

Sitrof soon came to the same realization. The two friends looked at each other and started laughing. They laughed because they were so happy they were both still alive and unharmed. Not many on that planet lived after taking part in a grueling battle like the one they had just had, and no one had lived after going toe to toe with Mandar before.

Just then, their laughter stopped as they heard Mandar's voice to their left. "I hate to break up this moment of bonding, but it is time for you both to die. And this time, neither one of you will come back," Mandar said.

"Why don't you just call it a day and get out of here already?" Christopher said.

"Because," Mandar said with an evil tone, "this time, I have something you want."

Christopher and Sitrof looked in disbelief as Mandar held up the crystal cross in his evil hand. A horrible feeling came over Christopher upon seeing Mandar holding his cross. It looked tiny in his massive hand.

Mandar then said, "As much as I hate and despise you believers, I have seen some powerful magic come out of this thing today. A magic that will be put to much better use in my control."

"It won't do you any good, Mandar. The power of that cross cannot be used for evil or to attack people," Christopher said.

"You were probably just too weak and stupid to know how to use it the right way, you pathetic little wimp!" Mandar shouted.

"First of all, if I am a pathetic little wimp, how come I was able to just beat you? How was I able to leave you lying there unconscious like a pile of trash waiting for the garbage man?" Christopher said.

Mandar looked at Christopher in confusion.

Sitrof looked confused as well and said, "Um, Chris, what was that supposed to mean? What's a garbage man?"

"Never mind. I'm just trash-talking him," Christopher replied.

"What is trash-talking? Is that when the garbage man speaks?"

"No, trash talk is sort of like an insult on my planet. You try to get into your opponent's head. It's the first thing that came to my mind, so I said it. I'm tired, I guess. Not my best insult."

"But what's a garbage man?" Sitrof asked.

"I'll explain it to ya later," Christopher said.

"Shut up, both of you!" Mandar screamed, frustrated by how annoying he found the two friends. "It's time to end this."

Mandar held the cross with his muscular arm outstretched, directing it toward Christopher and Sitrof. "Attack them," Mandar demanded of the crystal cross.

Nothing happened. The power in the cross remained dormant. Mandar looked down at the cross with an aggravated expression. He tried shaking the cross as if it needed a jolt to wake up. "I said attack them!"

Again, nothing happened. The light in the crystal cross would not show itself.

"I told you, man. The power can't be used to attack or for doing evil things," Christopher said.

Mandar was now enraged, as he felt he was making a fool out of himself. His pride was hurt when what Christopher had said proved to be correct. For a warrior like Mandar, having one's pride insulted was never a good thing.

Mandar heard rumblings from his army as they watched. He heard some of them say he probably was not worthy to use the weapon since he had been defeated. Others said maybe Mandar should no longer be their leader since he had lost in battle to a small believer.

Mandar became even more determined to make the cross do his evil bidding. He felt that once the army saw him wield the new alien power, they would have no choice but to fear and obey him again.

Mandar held the cross with both hands directly above his head. "I command you to obey me. Work for me now!" he shouted with great authority.

Suddenly, the crystal cross lit up. Christopher and Sitrof looked on in fear and horror, feeling sick in the pits of their stomachs. They wondered how Mandar had gotten the cross to work for him. They feared the damage Mandar could do with the power of the cross at his disposal. He had conquered everyone he had battled up until that day, but with the cross's power, he would be completely unstoppable.

The warriors watching from a distance focused their full attention on what was happening. Some wondered what Mandar would do with his new power, and others hoped that Mandar hadn't heard the disrespectful comments they had made about him.

The light from the crystal cross filled the sky, shining brightly above Mandar's powerful head. An eerie, evil smirk came over his battle-scarred face as he realized the amazing power was finally obeying his command.

The light from the cross grew wider and wider in diameter above Mandar's head. It extended ten feet in all directions, reaching out from the center of the cross, forming a massive circle above Mandar. Christopher and Sitrof took a few steps backward out of fear of the massive amount of energy the cross was producing. The ends of the circle then shot downward toward the ground, forming a circle from sky to ground directly around Mandar. The circle began moving in closer and closer to the power-hungry Mandar.

"Yes! Fill me with the power!" Mandar said as the giant circle of light closed in on him.

The enormous circle began spinning. Faster and faster it spun, forming a force field around Mandar. The light was so bright that Christopher and Sitrof had to shield their eyes from the blinding rays. The light from the cross completely engulfed the massive warrior, as it had Sitrof earlier. No one outside that circle could see Mandar anymore. He was completely covered by the brightness, as if it were swallowing him.

Though Christopher and Sitrof could no longer see Mandar, they could hear him yelling and screaming. They were unable to tell the cause of the screams or if they were screams of pain or roars of evil joy. The minds of the two believers raced. Was Mandar growing even bigger and stronger after being engulfed by the light? Was he being killed or punished by the light? What was happening?

One more bright flash shot out from the force field surrounding Mandar, forcing Sitrof and Christopher to turn completely around so their backs were to the cross. Then, as quickly as the light had started, it disappeared.

Christopher and Sitrof turned back around and saw Mandar sitting there on his knees with the cross in his hand. Christopher and Sitrof looked at each other with confusion, wondering what was coming next. Mandar was smiling, which made the two friends worry that he had gotten exactly what he was looking for: absolute power.

Mandar stood up slowly, smiling all the while. The smile then faded as his expression became more serious. He looked around as if taking everything in. He looked first at Sitrof, then at Christopher, then at his army, and then, lastly, back down at the cross in his massive hand. Mandar then started walking toward Sitrof and Christopher.

The two friends got into fighting positions as Mandar approached them. He looked different to them, as if the great warrior were now even more confident or fearless in some way. That made Christopher nervous. What was Mandar going to do? What was his attack going to be?

When Mandar stood only a few feet from them, Sitrof and Christopher noticed that his face wasn't bruised or bleeding anymore. There were no cuts or scratches of any kind on his face or body to indicate he had just been in a life-or-death battle. Then, suddenly, Mandar spoke.

"I am so sorry!" Mandar said humbly with tears flowing down his face. He stared down at the ground as he spoke.

Christopher and Sitrof looked at each other again, more confused than ever.

Mandar continued. "How can I ever make up for what I have done? How can I ever make it up to this world? But more importantly, how can I make it up to the two of you? Please, I beg you. Please forgive me. I did not know what I was doing."

"What are you talking about?" Christopher asked, puzzled.

"Here. This belongs to you." Mandar held out the cross to Christopher. "I asked it to fill me with power, and it definitely did. But it sure wasn't the type of power I was expecting."

Christopher carefully took the crystal cross from Mandar's outstretched hand, as he wasn't sure if Mandar was playing a trick or game of some kind with him. "What do you mean? What type of power did it fill you with?" Christopher asked, even more perplexed now.

Sitrof jumped in to answer the question. "The power of Jesus. The cross filled you with the power and love of Jesus, didn't it, Mandar?"

"Yes, it did," Mandar said. "And I am so ashamed that I rejected his love for all these years. Ashamed of all the people I've hurt and killed, especially the ones I hurt simply because they knew what I did not. That Jesus is life. People like you, Sitrof. People who never did me any harm but who I wanted to destroy because they were different. I cannot even begin to fathom all the hurt I have caused, but I know all I can do is ask for forgiveness, starting with you. Please forgive me." Mandar got down on his knees. "Please, Sitrof, forgive me. I beg of you."

"Mandar, please rise off of your knees. If the Lord Jesus has forgiven you by showing you the way, who am I to act any differently? I without question forgive you," Sitrof said with a sincere and gracious smile.

Christopher was both astonished and bewildered by what he was witnessing. He couldn't believe how easily Sitrof had forgiven Mandar after they had spent years as mortal enemies. After years of being hunted and in constant fear for his life, Sitrof had forgiven him as if nothing had ever happened between the two of them. Had Sitrof forgotten that just a few minutes ago, he had been killed at the hands of Mandar? How could he be so forgiving so quickly? Christopher knew that Mandar's apology was sincere and without an ulterior motive, but he was still skeptical. Even if Mandar had completely changed, it was because of the power of the cross, so how could Sitrof have had such an immediate change of heart toward such a terrorizing adversary?

Then it dawned on Christopher as if he were seeing clearly for the first time. Sitrof was simply following the example of Jesus and living the example. Unlike many who pretended to follow the Word of God, Sitrof truly was following it without any questions asked. Christopher realized Sitrof knew that if Jesus had not wanted Mandar forgiven, the crystal cross could have just killed him or sent him away. Instead, it had shown him the light, the way, and the truth. Sitrof saw that, and he had acted accordingly without hesitation.

Christopher then thought about how far humans would have to go before they were at that level. On Earth, if someone had tried to kill Christopher, he wouldn't have forgiven the person based on a simple apology. Yet Sitrof, who had grown up on a planet where believing in Jesus could get one killed, followed Jesus's beliefs and teachings to the fullest. Christopher felt embarrassed, for just a few hours ago, he hadn't even believed in what he now knew was true. *Jesus is the Son of God, and Jesus is love!* Christopher then had another realization. He finally understood why the cross wouldn't attack Mandar when the battle with him began. The power of the cross had known it was Mandar's destiny to see the way. It had been his destiny to come to Jesus. The whole battle had been a classroom set up for Mandar to learn and for the army of warriors to witness a lesson about sacrifice, forgiveness, love, and, above all, God.

"Christopher, I know I have no right to ask this, but can you forgive me for what I have done?" Mandar said.

Christopher looked up at Mandar's sincere face, a face that had previously been filled only with anger and rage. It now seemed to exude nothing but peace and calm.

"Yes, Mandar, I forgive you. It goes against every instinct I have, because I am not as quick to forgive as Sitrof is. I come from a very skeptical world, where basically, your actions speak louder than your words. You must continue to prove that you want to make up for the way you have acted in the past for the rest of your life."

"I totally agree. In fact, I would like to join you, Sitrof. I would like to join you on your mission to spread the Word of Jesus throughout our world. It's so strange. I used to wage war for fun and not even think twice about it. But now I can see the face of every person I have hurt. Every building I have destroyed. Every family I tore apart. I think I must spread the Word of Jesus for at least ten lifetimes to make up for the amount of people I have hurt. But I'm not complaining. I'm ready for the challenge if you'll help me, Sitrof," Mandar said.

"I would be happy to have you by my side. You've been a great warrior your whole life. Now it's time for you to be a warrior for God," Sitrof said.

"Christopher, will you be staying here with us?" Mandar asked.

"No, I have my own planet to get back to and my own path to

follow. But I think the two of you are going to do a lot of good here. Who knows? Maybe someday I'll come back, and this planet will be full of peace," Christopher said with a smile of hope.

"Well, let's not go too far there. Including Mandar and myself, there are still only about thirty-six believers left on the entire planet," Sitrof said.

"True. But if my memory serves me right, Jesus only had twelve disciples on my planet. How many did he have here?" Christopher asked.

"The same number: twelve. Why do you ask?" Sitrof said.

"Because the way I see it, he gave you a lot more followers to build off of than he had, and I have to believe that others are going to convert into believers after what they witnessed here," Christopher said with a smile as he pointed at the crowd of soldiers, who were still standing behind the wall of light.

Some of the soldiers had already dispersed, for they had seen Mandar be defeated and become a believer, and they viewed it as an opportunity to take his place. They already had left to seize power and create their own armies. But as Christopher had said, perhaps some of the others who were still there were open to the idea of believing after what they had seen. Sitrof and Mandar both turned and looked at the soldiers and smiled, for they knew that some of them could be the beginning of a new alliance of believers.

"You know something? For a young creature, you make a lot of sense," Mandar said, nodding in agreement.

Sitrof stood there smiling as Mandar spoke. He was proud of the two men he could now call his friends, and that made him happy.

"Well, I know you can't stay, Chris, but I wish you could," Sitrof said. "It has been an honor to fight by your side. I know on your planet, you must be someone of great importance."

"Actually, no, I'm not at all. I'm just your average kid there," Christopher replied.

"Give it time, young one. Give it time. You may not be important now, but you will be," Sitrof said matter-of-factly.

Christopher just nodded as if to say thank you. The three of them turned and walked toward the shoreline. Before they walked off together, Christopher looked back at the remaining crowd and held up the crystal cross for them to appreciate. Many of them cheered at the sight. The wall of light stayed up until Christopher, Mandar, and Sitrof were safely out of sight. Then, once they were gone, the wall of light vanished in front of the eyes of the crowd. Some of them walked down to investigate the spots where events that could only have been described as miracles had taken place. Seeing Sitrof brought back to life and Mandar reborn had changed some of them permanently.

As the three new friends continued walking along the shoreline, Christopher told them about Mike, his journey, and how he had gotten there. He told them what he had seen on the other planet, Ragor, and all the amazing things the crystal cross had done. He also explained that he had to get back to the meeting place to meet Mike so he could go home. They stopped and turned to look at the large black ocean waves crashing down.

Mandar said, "You know, I never really looked at how beautiful the ocean is."

"Everything God created has beauty; some of it is just harder to see," Sitrof responded.

Out of nowhere, someone jumped out and tackled Christopher to the ground. It was Allanac, who had been left unconscious earlier in the battle. He was now awake and ready to fight.

The impact of Allanac's crushing blindside tackle and the fall to the ground caused Christopher to lose his grip on the cross. It bounced on the ground and then rolled down the gravel of the shoreline. Christopher reached for it, but it slid down too fast. In the blink of an eye, it fell into the black ocean, and a forty-foot wave swallowed it. Christopher looked in horror as the crystal cross disappeared into the blackness forever. "No!" he screamed out in fear and anguish.

Allanac then put Christopher in a choke hold and started applying pressure. "Mandar, I got him for you! You take care of Sitrof, and I'll take care of this one!" he shouted to his master.

Sitrof and Mandar ran to Christopher's rescue. Mandar got there first. He pulled Allanac off Christopher and yelled, "What are you doing?" He held his soldier up in the air with one arm.

"I'm doing what you wanted us to do, Mandar. Kill the small creature so you can kill Sitrof," Allanac answered, confused as to why he was being questioned for following orders.

Sitrof reached Christopher and helped him to his feet.

"I was wrong, Allanac. There is no longer a reason to hurt them. There is no longer a reason to hurt anyone," Mandar said, still holding the soldier in the air.

"What do you mean? What have they done to you, Master?"

"They have done nothing except show me the truth—that's all. I can now see clearly for the first time in my life."

"No, Master. They must have you under a spell or something. Let me go so I can kill them. And then the spell will be broken, and you will return to your normal self," Allanac said.

"You will not kill anyone ever again, Allanac. That is an order," Mandar said.

Allanac kicked Mandar in the stomach to get away from his grip. He turned to him and said, "I don't take orders from you anymore. You have turned soft. When we meet again, I'll have my own soldiers who answer to me. And I will make sure you are destroyed."

With that, Allanac ran off into the distance. Even though Allanac had lost his respect for Mandar, he still knew he was no match for him in a battle. He would build a new alliance of his own.

Mandar wanted to chase him down and strangle him for threatening to destroy him and calling him soft.

Sitrof saw the frustration in Mandar's face and gently put his hand on his shoulder. "Jesus said you can be a hero except in your own country. Basically, for you, Mandar, that means the ones who knew you best will have the hardest time believing you have changed. And they will also be your biggest obstacles and enemies moving forward. You have to get used to it because each one of them, especially the ones who took orders from you, will try to lure you into a fight, as Allanac just did. All it takes is one moment of weakness to head back down the path you were on before. Don't let anyone do that to you."

Mandar nodded to show he understood. Then he looked sad for a moment. "I have to wonder. Was Allanac always like that, or did I make him that way?" Mandar asked.

"We all choose who we want to become, Mandar. Sure, there are variables that help us to make that choice, but the choice is still ours. Free will, remember? Allanac is who he wants to be, and now you are who you want to be. Maybe one day he will come around, as you have. For his sake, I hope he does," Sitrof said.

Mandar suddenly turned to make sure Christopher was all right. Christopher was just standing there staring at the black ocean. "Chris, are you okay?" Mandar asked.

"No, I'm anything but okay. The cross fell into the ocean. It's gone. It's gone forever. I can't even go in there to try to look for it," Christopher said.

"Well, you can't, but we can. We can swim in this ocean," Sitrof said.

"Thanks, but let's be realistic. Do you think we are ever going to find it with the size of those waves? It's probably miles away from here already," Christopher said with frustration.

"We have to try. We won't know until we try, right?" Mandar said, trying to express his newfound feeling of hope for all situations.

Christopher forgot about the cross for a moment and marveled at the change in Mandar. This creature that had been so evil before was now as innocent as a little boy. He just wanted to help his new friend in any way he could.

Christopher turned to Mandar and said, "Thank you for pulling Allanac off of me. I really appreciate it. Remember that moment. It was your first good deed." Christopher laughed.

Mandar smiled. "Yes, you are right. It was my first good deed. And I didn't even think twice about doing it. That's a good sign, right?" he said, looking for approval.

"Yes, it's a great sign—very encouraging. But remember, we don't do good deeds to make ourselves feel better. We do them simply because they are the right thing to do. The fact that you acted without thinking shows that you knew it was right. That's the truly encouraging part," Sitrof said.

"Way to go, Mandar. I'm proud of you," Christopher said. "Now, how in the world am I going to get home? No offense, but I can't be stuck here. I have a life on my own planet. People who love me are waiting for me. I have to get back to them. It's almost Christmas."

All of a sudden, a voice came from above them. It said, "Fear not, Christopher, for it is the power that brought you here, and it is the power that will bring you back home."

"I know that voice. That's Mike!" Christopher shouted happily.

Mike suddenly appeared, standing right behind Christopher, Sitrof, and Mandar. They all quickly turned and saw him standing there. Sitrof and Mandar couldn't believe their eyes. They were as shocked as Christopher had been the first time Mike had appeared out of nowhere in front of him. Even though Christopher had explained about Mike to them, they almost hadn't believed it was true until now. Mike walked over to Sitrof first.

"It's good to see you alive and well, Sitrof. Be more careful. This world needs you," Mike said with a smile and a nod. Sitrof smiled back at him.

Mike then walked to Mandar. "Mandar, it's great to see you on the good side for a change. You've found your way home. Now, try not to stray from your course again. It takes a brave person to change. Stay with Sitrof, and you'll be fine," he said with another nod and smile. Mandar nodded humbly back at him.

"Mike, I lost the cross in the ocean. It's gone. How am I going to get home?" Christopher said almost frantically.

Mike turned to Christopher with a smile. "It's good to see you too, Chris. I'm glad to see you haven't lost your sense of panic." He laughed.

"How can you make jokes now? This is serious, Mike. The cross is lost," Christopher said sternly.

"Kid, have you learned nothing from this whole experience?" Mike asked.

"No, I've learned a lot, actually. But what does that have to do with me losing the cross? I've lost the power you trusted to me, so now what am I going to do?"

"Chris, the power is within you," Mike said.

"What do you mean? I don't understand."

"The power of Jesus is within everyone who believes in him. Look at the change in Mandar if you need proof of that. Your cross was simply a tool so you could see the power at work. Like we determined on the football field back on Earth, you needed to see something in order for it to be real. Remember?"

Mandar turned to Sitrof and asked, "What's a football field?"

Sitrof shrugged his muscular shoulders to signify that he didn't know either.

Mike continued. "All you have to do is ask for the cross back, and it will come back to you if that is what you want."

Christopher turned and looked at the massive ocean. Another wave crashed down with a thunderous roar. He thought hard about his crystal cross and how much he wanted it back.

Mike turned to Sitrof and Mandar and said with a smile, "You guys might want to watch this. It's gonna be cool!"

Christopher continued to concentrate, staring into the endless black of the mighty ocean. He heard Mike's voice in his head: *Have faith, Christopher. Believe.*

Christopher concentrated even harder. He did have faith. He did believe. His eyes seemed to be drawn to a part of the ocean that was at least a mile away from shore, past all the fifty-foot breaking waves. He didn't know why his eyes were drawn to that spot, but he knew he couldn't look away either. Then a shining light came shooting out of that spot. The light went straight up into the sky above the ocean. It seemed to be lighting up the black ocean from underneath the water's surface. It was as if the world's largest flashlight had just been turned on underneath the water. All of the waves suddenly dropped down at the same time, and the angry ocean was quiet and still. The seemingly infinite blackness of the water lit up as far as their eyes could see. Suddenly, right at the spot Christopher's eyes had gravitated to, the crystal cross burst out of the ocean water, glowing at full strength.

Mike looked over at Sitrof and Mandar, who stood in awe with their mouths wide open, as they had never seen anything like that. Mike elbowed Sitrof softly in the ribs and said with a smile, "Didn't I tell you it was gonna be cool?"

Sitrof couldn't even respond. He was mesmerized by the beautiful sight of the ocean lighting up as far as he could see. The cross continued shooting upward out of the ocean, still glowing, fully lit. Once it reached its pinnacle high above the ocean, it stopped and hovered in midair. It floated over the motionless, illuminated water for a few seconds so that all could see it. The cross then flew through the air toward shore and toward Christopher.

Christopher didn't know what to say. He was in shock, just as Sitrof and Mandar were. The cross finally came to rest in the palm of Christopher's hand. The light dimmed, the ocean turned black again, and the waves once again crashed down. Christopher turned around and looked at Mike in disbelief.

Mike just stood there proudly, smiling from ear to ear. "Chris, nothing is impossible with God," he said, being serious for a moment.

"Wait a minute. Mike? As in Michael?" Sitrof asked.

"Yeah, why?" Christopher asked. He hadn't realized that since the cross was still translating for the different aliens, the name of Michael had been translated in Sitrof's language and was a name he had heard of before.

"Dear Lord, you are the angel Michael, aren't you? The archangel? The protector? The warrior? That is you, isn't it?" Sitrof asked excitedly.

"Wow, you know your history, huh?" Mike said in jest.

"You were a warrior?" Mandar asked, interested to hear that even a messenger and angel of God could be a warrior.

"Yes, Mandar. Even the good guys need warriors. That is why you are so important. The battle between good and evil is a constant one. The more warriors we have on our side the better. While fighting or battling is never a desired option, it is sometimes a necessary outcome when a powerful evil leaves no other alternative," Mike said.

Just then, a noise startled them. A small number of Mandar's army walked directly up to them and lined up in front of Mandar and Sitrof with their weapons in their hands. They all looked at each other and then threw their weapons down onto the ground. Each warrior then got down on one knee. One of them spoke. He asked if they could be allowed to join Sitrof and Mandar wherever they went. He said they could not ignore what they had witnessed, and they wanted to learn more about God, Jesus, and the significance of the cross.

Sitrof and Mandar accepted their offer, and Sitrof also promised to explain the teachings of Jesus to all of them. A new alliance had now been formed, but it was unlike any the planet had seen in quite some time. The members of this alliance could inspire hope and change wherever they went. Rather than spreading more destruction and death, as the other alliances in the area did, they could spread the Word and do good works.

Sitrof beamed at the thought of the opportunity they had to make a difference for the better. Mike and Christopher just stood there smiling.

Mike then turned to Christopher. "So, kid, are you ready to go home now?"

"More than you know!" Christopher said with a smile.

"Well, come on then. Let's go."

Christopher looked at Sitrof and Mandar, two beings who had been opponents for years but now were allies. What a miracle that Mandar, a being filled with hatred, had changed to be filled with love and that Sitrof, a being who had been hunted and persecuted, had been so willing to forgive and move on. How could Christopher ever put into words what he had witnessed that night? He slowly walked over to Sitrof, and the two gave each other a well-deserved hug.

"My dad told me earlier today that miracles still happen every day, but most people don't take the time to recognize them. I will never forget all the miracles I saw on this day, and I hope you won't either. I am so grateful I got to meet you, know you, fight beside you, and learn from a person with as much faith as you. I will never forget you, Sitrof," Christopher said to his larger-than-life friend.

"Nor will I forget you. It was an honor and a privilege to meet you, my young friend. It was God's will that we met on this day, and I am honored to have played a part in your journey. Thank you for everything," Sitrof said.

The two friends embraced once more for a final goodbye. The bond they had developed that night would last throughout their lives.

Christopher then turned to Mandar to give him a hug, but rather than hugging Christopher, Mandar picked him up and squeezed him with affection.

"Thank you, my young friend. Thank God for bringing you here," Mandar said as he gently put Christopher down.

"Thank you, Mandar. I'm so glad I got to witness your change. I thought I would leave this planet having nightmares of you, but now I will hopefully only have fond memories of you. You give me hope for some people on my planet. Keep the faith, and whenever you start to have doubts, remember everything about this day, okay?" Christopher said.

"Yes, I will. I will never forget you. I never thought I would look so fondly upon the person who finally defeated me in battle. I also never thought I would win so much in losing my first fight," Mandar said with a smile that almost made Christopher forget how menacing he used to look.

Christopher took a few steps toward Mike but then turned back to the two inhabitants of that planet. He saw two former enemies who were now brothers in a cause. He also looked at the group of former warriors standing behind them, waiting to be led and begin their new journey of faith. Christopher said, "I have a feeling the two of you working together will be able to do a lot of good here. Good luck, and may God continue to bless you both."

The two nodded back at Christopher. Christopher then turned and walked back over to Mike. "I'm ready now," he said.

"Okay, just click your heels together three times, and say, 'There's no place like home.'"

"What?" Christopher asked.

"I'm just kidding. I just always wanted to use that on someone," Mike said with his infectious smile.

Mandar and Sitrof once again looked at each other, confused, as they did not get the *Wizard of Oz* reference.

Christopher saw that the two giants didn't understand and quickly said, "Don't worry, guys. You aren't missing anything; it was just a bad attempt at a joke." He laughed, looking in Mike's direction.

"Hey, be careful, Chris. You aren't home just yet," Mike said in jest.

Christopher smiled at Mike and then looked down at his cross. The crystal cross started to glow in his hand. Christopher once again felt everything start to spin around him. Unlike before, this time, he knew what was happening, and he smiled and clutched the cross as tightly as he could. Sitrof and Mandar stood there watching from a distance and waving goodbye to him. Their new followers, their disciples, also watched, witnessing yet another miracle on that day. Suddenly, the glowing cross pulled Christopher upward into the planet's yellow sky, and in the blink of an eye, he was gone.

Sitrof and Mandar stood there looking up. They could see only a white dot moving farther and farther away from them. "I'm really going to miss him," Sitrof said.

"Don't worry; you have me now," Mandar joked.

They turned to look at Mike, but they were too late; he had vanished while they were watching Christopher fly off into the sky. The two new friends turned and walked off together, with their followers walking with them. They started talking about what they had witnessed that day and agreed they needed to write it all down so that no detail was overlooked. They had seen an alien from another planet, filled with the power of Jesus in a crystal cross. They had seen Sitrof get struck down and die, only to be brought back to life by the cross. They had seen Mandar's heart softened and the change within him. They had seen the crystal cross light up the entire ocean, stopping the massive waves, to fly from out at sea back to the hand of its alien owner onshore.

None of them knew what lay ahead for them in the future, but with a renewed and unwavering faith, they were willing to meet the challenges. After everything they had witnessed, they knew that whatever happened, there was one truth they would never forget: Jesus was by their side always.

CHAPTER 10

A New Outlook

CHRISTOPHER ONCE AGAIN HAD NO
control over where or in which direction the cross went, but
this time, he knew where he was going to end up. He was on his way
home, and he was excited to get there.

He moved through space again, passing the same stars, planets,
and galaxies he had passed before, only in reverse. The big white glow
again surrounded him, protecting him from the dangers of space.
He knew he was again moving faster than the speed of light, but
for some reason, he was able to enjoy it more this time. His feeling
of uncertainty regarding what was happening to him was gone. He
could just sit back, enjoy the ride, and recognize the miracles in what
he was seeing.

Christopher was coming up to the Milky Way galaxy. The
experience of going into it was different from coming out of it. He
knew what he was flying into and could truly enjoy and appreciate
everything he saw. He again saw Pluto and Neptune, and then he
got to see the beautiful rings of Saturn for a second time up close.
He passed all the moons of Jupiter and saw the gigantic red spot the
planet was famous for. He passed Mars, and then he saw the little

blue marble called Earth once again. His speed decreased. He flew past the Sea of Tranquility on the side of the moon. The cross all of a sudden stopped glowing, and Christopher came to a sudden halt. He hovered there in space, and when he looked down below his dangling Nike sneakers, right below him was his beautiful home planet of Earth.

It looked much more beautiful after he had worried he would never see it again. The planet looked so peaceful from that distance. He could not see any wars being fought. He could not see any crimes being committed. He could not see people stealing or killing in the streets. He could not hear people arguing, shouting, or hurting each other. He could not see anyone dying from disease. He could not hear people mourning loved ones who had passed away. He thought about how those negative things reminded him of Sitrof's planet, and he worried that Earth could one day end up like that.

But then he realized that from that distance, he couldn't see or hear the positive things either. He couldn't hear people laughing and having fun. He couldn't see newborn babies full of the promise of a bright future. He couldn't hear children playing and making new friends. He couldn't see people falling in love and getting married. He couldn't see fathers and sons playing catch in their backyards. He couldn't hear mothers and daughters sharing special moments. He couldn't see the random acts of kindness that happened every day. He couldn't hear people praying together to get through tough times. Christopher then thought about how all of those positive things reminded him of Ragor's planet, and he wondered if Earth could possibly end up like that one day.

The three planets he had been on were similar in some ways yet far apart in others. Christopher thought that from that distance, all three looked exactly the same. What the inhabitants of each planet chose to do with what they had was what made them so different. Ragor's planet was full of love and faith, Sitrof's planet was full of hate and despair, and Christopher's planet lay somewhere in the middle. He was grateful to see Earth and all its beauty again and couldn't wait to be home.

"Thank you, God, for bringing me home," Christopher said.

The crystal cross then lit up again and pulled him down into the beautiful blue, green, and white planet. Once again, the white glow of the cross surrounded him like a cocoon. Christopher was almost disappointed that the glow was all he could see around him. He wanted to see all the skyscrapers and clouds as he flew downward.

Then the white glow vanished, and the light of the cross was extinguished. Christopher had safely landed feet first right in the football stadium where his journey had begun. Mike appeared next to him almost immediately.

"All right, Christopher, your journey is almost complete," Mike said. "What have you learned tonight?"

"Wow, now, that's a question. Where do I even start to begin to describe what I saw and learned on this journey?" Christopher replied.

"Just speak from your heart, and say whatever comes to mind."

"Well, I learned that there is definitely life on other planets, but more importantly, there is a God, and his Son is named Jesus. And Jesus didn't visit and sacrifice himself on this planet to save only it from sin but to save all life in the universe. I learned that good and evil aren't limited to the human race. I also learned that it's never too late for a person to change. But can I ask you something? If Jesus visited all three of the planets I have seen, including Earth, why are they all so different?"

"Well, I know you were just thinking about this as you hovered above Earth before coming back down to the ground. Let's start with the obvious. You saw one planet where the people have almost completely embraced the message of Jesus and then one planet where the people have almost completely rejected the message. You saw the outcomes of both choices made by the people of those planets. You saw the rewards and also the consequences of those choices," Mike said.

"But what about Earth?"

"Well, Chris, Earth can still go either way. Remember, free will was given to you by God. The power to choose is an awesome power, and it's a responsibility that sometimes is taken for granted. It's up to you as a people to determine which way you are going to go. The message has been delivered. It's up to each individual to make the choice to either accept or reject the Word."

"So you mean I was right, and Earth could still end up like Sitrof and Mandar's planet?"

"Yes, it could. Look at how many wars your planet has already gone through in its relatively short existence. You've even had numerous wars supposedly in the name of God. I want to know why any religious leader of any planet would think his or her God wanted people killed in dedication to him. To think that God would want his creatures killed simply for not believing in him—that is the strangest thing I've ever heard, and I've been around a long time. Why would he have given people free will if they would just be forced to worship him? God wants people to choose to love and worship him. His love is unconditional to us, but lucky for us, he does not expect or require the same. That is also why Earth could still end up like Ragor's planet as well. He wants love and peace for all of his creatures. Is there death for all life on this planet? Yes, but that is what a mortal life entails. Are there unfair things that happen here? Yes, but sometimes those are also a consequence of free will. And remember, a mortal death here on your planet is not a permanent one, for your life and soul live on," Mike said.

"I am so sorry for ever having the doubts I had. After everything I've seen tonight, I feel ashamed for ever feeling that way," Christopher said, looking down at the ground.

"Don't be ashamed, Chris. Lots of good people have feelings of doubt. Doubts are normal. The trick is to not let the doubts consume you. People make the mistake of letting fear, doubt, and worry take over their lives. Worrying is simply praying in reverse. It's taking energy that could be spent in a positive way and using it negatively in a way that drains the happiness out of you. Make sure a moment of doubt is nothing more than that: just a moment. Remember that, and you'll be fine. That's why you were chosen for this trip. You have a big future ahead of you if you make the right choices."

"Mike, I do have to ask this: Why me? I mean, why was I lucky enough to be the only one to have seen what you showed me tonight?"

"What makes you think you are the only one?" Mike said with a smirk.

"You mean there are others who have had this kind of journey?"

"Sure, there have been quite a few over the centuries. There have been journeys by humans to other planets as well as by beings from other planets to Earth. Most of the time, when you see shooting stars, they are just shooting stars, but sometimes those shooting stars are beings being transported the same way you were."

"So that's why I was surrounded by the white light each time I went in and out of a planet? So that I looked like a shooting star? Amazing. I can't believe there are others who have experienced journeys like this."

"Well, they all are told the same thing I'm about to tell you. You cannot talk about it. That's the rule. This journey was for you and you alone. You can share some of the things you learned, but you can never talk about how you learned them. Understand?"

"Yes, I understand. Besides, who would ever believe me anyway?" Christopher said jokingly.

"All right, Christopher, it's been a pleasure being your guide. You showed maturity and bravery well beyond your years in some very unpleasant and unpredictable situations. Without you, Sitrof could have died, and Mandar may never have found the Lord. Be proud not only of what you have seen but also of what you have done. Most importantly, remember that this wasn't a one-night journey. The journey of faith is a lifelong journey, one in which you will constantly learn and understand more by the day. Don't ever become content with your journey and start thinking you've learned enough or have all the answers. When people decide to stop learning and stop wanting to understand, they then take their first steps off the path and begin to lose their way. It's very dangerous when people start to feel they know all they need to know or have all the answers. Don't ever think you know all the answers, because you don't.

"Another thing that will help you is to remember what we talked about during our first conversation together. When I asked how you feel when people don't like football, you responded by saying they never gave it a chance or enough time to understand. I tell you to remember that because people tend to judge things before they take the time to understand them completely. That is especially true when discussing faiths or religions. People sometimes make their decisions without taking the time to really try to understand things. Even you were guilty of having doubts, so my advice to you is to be patient when talking to others who have the same doubts you did or have different outlooks than you do. Perhaps you can help influence them, but you can't force them to believe. It is their free will, and you can only try to help be a guide to others. You can't insist that people feel the same way you do or believe the same things you believe. You just be the best you that you can be, and lead by example. Hopefully others are drawn to you, and you can help them. You have seen a lot on this night, and hopefully you will remember these lessons forever. Always trust your gut, and you won't go wrong. Okay?"

"Yes. Thank you, Mike. I'll always remember everything about this journey, and I'll try to remember everything I learned from you and to live up to being worthy of this journey. Words can't express how grateful and humbled I am to have been given this opportunity."

"I'm glad, kid, and again, I'm happy I got to be your guide. Now, just walk over to the middle of the field, and stand on the big *C* logo. You will then be transported safely back to the bedroom of your house."

"Thank you again for everything. I'm glad you were my guide too. I will never forget you."

"Well, I should hope not," Mike said with his trademark smirk and sarcastic sense of humor. "Now, go ahead home. You have a family waiting for you who love you and need you."

"Will I ever see you again?" Christopher asked.

"One day, kid. I guarantee it," Mike said.

"Oh, um, I feel like I should thank God and Jesus for this journey. I mean, I want to thank them and need to thank them. Thank them for this whole experience and for everything the cross did and for this whole night. How can I ever thank them so they know how honored and grateful I truly am?" Christopher asked.

"They already know, Chris. But if you truly want to thank them, just pray more and talk to them more. Prayers should not just be limited to church services, when you want something, or before you eat a meal. Your prayers can and should be a running conversation, a running dialogue of everything in your life. Prayers are your way of having a relationship with God, so if you truly want to thank them, keep that relationship strong, and keep the conversations flowing," Mike said.

Christopher nodded in agreement and smiled, as he looked forward to doing that. He would pray and talk more with God to build a stronger relationship with him. It sounded simple, but many people didn't do it. There were people who had no problem talking to their psychiatrists or their social media followers but didn't take the time to talk to God. They didn't take the time to talk to Jesus.

Christopher would not be one of those people, and he realized how great it was that something as small as a conversation could mean so much to God.

Christopher turned to walk toward the center of the field, carrying his cross in his hand. He turned around to give Mike a final wave goodbye and then continued walking. He stood right on the logo in the middle of the field, as Mike had instructed, and turned around to look at Mike one last time.

"Christopher, one more thing!" Mike yelled out. "Remember the lesson you learned here on this field when we were playing catch with the football. Every time you see a football or watch a game, think of the time we spent together here. Remember that just because you can't always see something doesn't mean it isn't real. You don't see wind, but you can definitely feel it. The way you feel about God and the way that makes you feel—those feelings are what count. Those feelings are truly real. And above all else, always remember this: *Christ* is not just the first six letters in your name; he also lives inside of you always! Take care, kid." Mike vanished permanently into the night air.

Christopher was sad to see Mike leave, but he had no time to think about that, as his crystal cross lit up for its final job of the night. Light shot out from the cross and formed a circle around the logo Christopher was standing on. Then the light spun around and around, faster and faster. Christopher lifted off the ground, just as he'd lifted off the floor in his bedroom. He then disappeared and was no longer in the stadium.

The next thing he knew, he was opening his eyes and waking up from what felt like a deep sleep. He looked around, trying to figure out what was going on. He was in his bedroom. He was home, safe in his bed. He sat up, trying to wrap his head around what had just happened. He looked to his left to gaze out the window and saw daylight shining through the blinds. The night was over, and a new morning had begun. He pulled the blanket off himself and saw he was still wearing his clothes. He looked over at his desk and saw the crystal cross sitting there, as it always had. He stood up from his bed and walked over to the desk. He picked up the cross and studied it as if he were seeing it for the first time.

"Could it have all just been a dream?" he asked himself.

He looked in the top drawer to see if the little box from Mike, which had started the whole adventure last night, was still there. That would prove it actually had happened. He searched in all the drawers but did not find the box. He looked around the floor to see if it was there somewhere but found nothing. Had it all just been a dream?

He looked in his mirror to see if he had any bruises or injuries on his face. He didn't, but then he remembered that the cross had already healed his wounds, so that didn't matter. There was no evidence of his bedroom being disrupted or things being out of place from the spinning last night. There was no evidence of the little box. The cross was there, but no magical light shone out of it.

"It all felt so real," he said to himself. He thought of Mike, Ragor, Sitrof, Mandar, and the Orgilep. Many images flashed through his mind. He remembered what Mike had said: *Feeling is believing.* Then he had an epiphany: this was another test. There was no evidence that his journey had been real, but why would there have been? Part of the journey had been for Christopher to relearn what faith was, and in that moment, he knew he had all the evidence he needed. He didn't need proof; he had his faith. He knew what had happened, and he knew it had been real. He also realized that even it hadn't been real, it wouldn't have mattered. Even if the places he had been and people he had met hadn't been real, that wouldn't have changed how he felt or what he had learned. He knew he had been given a message.

In keeping with his word, he knelt down on his knees next to the bed and started praying. He thanked God and Jesus for everything in his life, including his journey. He promised to pray more and talk with them more throughout each day in everything he did.

After a few more moments of prayer, Christopher stood up and walked back over to the cross on his desk. He picked it up again, put it to his lips, and kissed the cross to thank it as well. Christopher then remembered that it wasn't just any morning: it was Christmas Eve morning. He looked at the cross in his hand, smiled, and put it back on top of the desk, where it belonged. "Thank you, Lord Jesus. Merry Christmas," he said, looking at the cross.

Just as Christopher was turning away to grab his jacket, he thought he saw a quick ray of light flash at him from the cross. Was it a reflection of some kind shining on it? Or had the cross lit up one last time to say, "You're welcome"? Christopher chose to think it was the latter.

Christopher smiled, grabbed his wallet out of the desk drawer, and then ran down the stairs. His family was already up, and they were eating breakfast in the kitchen.

"Good morning, honey. You want some cereal or something?" Mary asked.

Christopher didn't reply. He just looked at his family as if he hadn't seen them in years. He smiled, walked right over to his mom, and gave her a huge hug. He said, "I love you, Mom. You truly are the best. Thank you for always making everything so perfect and special."

"Oh, Chris, I love you too," she replied. He hugged her again, and then she again asked if he wanted something to eat.

"No, thanks, Ma. I'm not hungry. Besides, I have to get to the mall. I have to finish my shopping," he replied.

"Well, do you need a ride?" she asked with a smile.

"No, Ma, I'm gonna run there. I feel like I have a lot of energy to burn," Christopher said as he bolted toward the front door. He then tapped his dad on the shoulder and said, "Love you too, Pops." He continued over to Joey. He picked Joey up out of his chair and held his little brother over his head. Joey giggled as Christopher said, "You're the best little brother anyone could ever have." He put his brother back down and then ran out of the house on a mission to get to the mall.

Mary looked at her husband with a surprised expression. "I wonder what got into him. Last night, he didn't even want to think about Christmas, and today he's running off first thing in the morning without eating just to finish shopping?"

"Teenagers, Mary. Don't try to understand them, or you'll go crazy," Michael said with a smile.

Christopher ran out the front door into the cold morning. He ran down the porch steps and jumped into the snow on the front lawn. He started laughing and making snow angels. He was happy to see his wonderful city again. He thought he should have been exhausted after the night he had just been through. After all, fighting aliens and flying across the universe were not exactly relaxing. But for some reason, he wasn't at all tired. He stood up and continued running down the street across the snow. He felt different that day. He felt rejuvenated.

Christopher had always felt pride in being a Chicagoan, but now he felt pride in being a human on Earth. He felt pride in his planet, as he knew what it could one day become. It could be as great as the first planet he had visited, Ragor's planet, or maybe even better. He felt proud that maybe he could somehow help in a small way with the challenge of getting the planet to that point. What a different way he had of looking at things now.

He suddenly stopped running and looked up at the crisp blue sky. The birds that hadn't flown south for the winter were flying high against the backdrop of puffy clouds and the yellow sun. Then he looked at the white snow that blanketed the frozen green grass. He was home, and he had never been so happy to see a cold, wintery day. He continued on toward the mall, his fast run slowing to a brisk walk. He admired everything from the trees to the cracked concrete in the sidewalk he was walking on. He was so focused on taking everything in that he didn't notice a car pull up slowly behind him. His friend Johnny was behind the wheel, and he pulled up alongside where Christopher was walking.

"Hey, Chris, where you walkin' to, man?" Johnny asked after rolling the window down.

"Yo, Johnny, what's up, man? I'm headin' up to the mall. Where you goin' in your mom's ride?"

"I'm goin' to the mall too. Jump in."

Christopher opened the passenger door and got into the car. He fastened his seat belt, and the two drove off together. Johnny gave Christopher a confused look and said, "Chris, what are you doing up so early? You're never up this early, man."

"I know, right? Let's just say I didn't get a lot of sleep last night," Christopher said.

"I was up pretty late last night too. I just couldn't sleep, ya know? It was one of those nights for me. Oh, but I saw the coolest thing."

"Yeah? What was that?" Christopher asked.

"Well, like I said, I couldn't sleep, so I was lying on my bed, listening to some music. I was looking out my window, and I saw the brightest shooting star I've ever seen in my life flying through the sky," Johnny said.

Christopher just smiled as he remembered what Mike had told him about shooting stars. He realized that Johnny might have seen him flying through the air with the light from the cross surrounding him. "That's pretty cool. I think I may have seen the same one," Christopher said with a smirk.

"Did you really? It's rare to see them in the city," Johnny said, realizing he might have never seen one before. Johnny then tilted his head as if confused. "Hey, um, whatcha goin' to the mall for? Weren't you just there yesterday?"

MICHAEL J. DISALVO

"Yeah, I was. But remember, I didn't get anything. I have to finish my shopping. I was in a messed-up mood yesterday, man, but I feel much better today. Things are much clearer."

"Yeah? Good! Because you were talkin' some crazy stuff yesterday about God and Christmas that I didn't like. You were startin' to worry me with how you were talking, like you were turning into some kind of serial killer or something," Johnny said, and the two friends laughed.

"Don't worry; I won't be climbing rooftops or anything. Like I said, I was just in a mood. You won't hear me talkin' that junk anymore. And you don't have to worry about me either. I had someone tell me that worrying is just praying in reverse, and I intend to remember that. I had a moment of doubt, but that's all it was. A moment." Christopher looked out the window with a smile.

"Worrying is praying in reverse, huh? I like that," Johnny said. "Who told you that?"

"A guy I met from out of town," Christopher replied with a smirk.

Johnny turned onto the next block, and the two teens saw a man walking along the sidewalk. The man was wearing a hooded jacket and had the hood over his head to protect himself from the frigid air. The man stopped walking and looked at the car as it drove past. The man smiled and then pulled the hood back from over his head. It was Mike. He stood there with a proud look on his face. As the car drove out of sight, he put his hood back on and started walking again. "That a boy, Chris. It's a new day for you. You found your faith. Now your journey has just begun," he said with a smile. "Merry Christmas!"

MICHAEL DISALVO is an author and poet who draws upon his personal life experiences as inspiration for his writing. Having always had a passion and interest in being an author, he studied creative writing in college and even worked as a book seller to be around the written word. He excelled in a career as an analyst, as he enjoyed working to find the hidden story behind every problem. Originally from Chicago, he is a die-hard fan of the city's sports teams. He is happily married to his high school sweetheart, and they live in South Florida with their dog, Jordan.

Printed in the United States
By Bookmasters